THE HOUSE OF SPARK

Luminita LaFlash

Charleston, SC
www.PalmettoPublishing.com

The House of Spark

Cover designed by Teresa Jenellen

The House of Spark is a work of fiction. Specific long-established public spaces, institutions, agencies are mentioned, but the people, places, organizations, and events are fictions and fabrications.

First Edition

Hardcover ISBN: 978-0-578-25460-9
Paperback ISBN: 978-0-578-25461-6
eBook ISBN: 978-0-578-25458-6

To my grandbaby Adrian.
From your struggles to healing,
your journey inspires our family and others.
Your courage and strength teach us to keep going
and don't give up no matter what life throws at us.

I love you with all my heart.

Grandma Lumi.

Author's Note

Romania is a unique country situated in the southeastern part of Central Europe. Her capital, Bucharest, was known as an exceedingly beautiful city—often called the "Little Paris of the East" because of the similarity of its architecture to the big Paris in France.

The House of Spark, a thrilling political novel, takes place historically in Romania in the late 1950s. At that time, the Soviet Union occupied Romania. The Communist regime seized power in the country after the forced abdication of the last king of Romania, Michael I. Following the Russian model, the new administration invented the Securitate—an instrument of control and manipulation of the population. During this period, Soviet-style economics, education, and culture influenced every country's sector. However, the Romanian people often raised their voices and fought against the dictatorship.

Though a work of fiction, this book is inspired by real people and events from my family history.

In 1989, after forty-two years, one of the blackest chapters in Romanian history—the Communist regime—was finally closed. Most everyone who survived this period knows what it means to live in fear, be lied to and betrayed, be deprived of material necessities and fundamental rights, and pretend by compulsion that all was joyful and bright. After decades of misery and fear, thousands of Romanian families, like ours, were brave and resilient enough to carry on.

Romanian students fought against the Soviet Communist occupation and regime–against those who tried to control people's thoughts and beliefs. Their bravery is a lesson to us all:

"Family need not be defined merely as those with whom we share blood but as those for whom we would give our blood"

(Charles Dickens, *Nicholas Nickleby*).

Chapter One

Bucharest, 1958.

Everyone had wanted to join the celebration on that sunny day in Bucharest. Even though many things had gone wrong and there were quite a few political discords, it was set aside. Optimistically people thought the beautiful weather was a sign of hope for the future. For miles, you could hear happy cheers and people celebrating joyfully amid a sea of flags. The President's car slowly made its way through the city's overcrowded streets.

From inside the car, Vlad Nicolaescu, the Communist leader of Romania, smiled and waved at onlookers. Police and the Securitate roamed the streets, making sure nothing happened. People stood shoulder to shoulder, barely able to wave the flags they were holding tight. Suddenly, the energy in the crowd shifted. A small woman dressed in black had dashed through the police line and in front of the president's car.

The tires screeched, and when the driver corrected the steering, they narrowly missed hitting a group of people who spilled off the crowded sidewalk. The President's car avoided hitting the small woman who stood in front of the vehicle.

A few of the Securitate guards accompanying the motorcade intervened right away and wrestled the woman to the ground while others ensured the president was safe. Her shawl fell to the ground during her struggle with the Securitate, unveiling her long blond hair. Under her blue eyes, she had dark black circles. Many people who saw her closely thought she looked possessed. It took them a minute to hear what she was saying since her speech was unclear and broken. Aside from that, they were enraged not only that a woman had disrupted the event for no good reason but that she could have been responsible for the deaths of people who weren't as foolish as she was acting. With a mix of shock and curiosity, people watched the drama unfold. The woman struggled against the iron grip of the guards, repeating, "Mr. President, sir! Mr. President! Please let me talk with you. Please, sir!"

"Shut up, or we'll shoot you!" a guard yelled at the woman.

She ignored him and continued her plea. The handcuffs started to cut into her skin. She was aware of the pain but kept yelling, trying to get the president's attention, turning her tears into a shout. "Mr. President, help me, please!" Her voice got louder as she struggled against the Securitate. She knew she only had seconds for him to hear her plea and maybe, just maybe, decide to help her.

"Mr. President, sir, please…"

The Securitate tried to clear the street for the president's car. The commotion was dying down as people nearby who'd seen what happened were standing there in disbelief. A few women were crying, and others stood with dumbfounded expressions. Their flags lowered, and they no longer thought about the celebration. The Securitate started to drag her away roughly. The woman continued her litany as she was being pulled away. "Just one moment, sir, please listen to me for a moment. Sir…"

The car was about to pull away when the president listened to the woman's sobbing pleas. Something she said made him stare at her and change his mind.

Unsure why this woman's request affected him so much, he bellowed; "Stop the car now!"

* * *

2

Bucharest, 1957 (one year earlier).

A line of people waited eagerly at the corner of Bulevardul Gheorghe Gheorghiu Dej for bus 136 to pull up. Just as Jenica stepped off the curb and into the crowded bus, he heard someone calling his name.

"Wait! I need to talk with you."

Jenica spun around, recognizing the voice of his friend Mircea. He shook his head, frustrated. "I've waited thirty minutes for this bus, and I don't know when the next one is coming. What's going on?"

Mircea smiled and reached into his pocket; he pulled out a white envelope and handed it to Jenica. "This is worth the wait," he said mysteriously.

Jenica was thoroughly confused. "Is this a bribe? What are you trying to get me to do?"

Mircea burst into laughter loudly, making the other bus riders stare. Jenica swallowed his embarrassment, accepted the envelope, and lifted open the flap.

"You snake!" he said and looked up, his eyes opening wide. "Where did you get these? How?"

Mircea looked smug. "Wasn't me. Doina is to blame. Have a good time."

There was barely a moment to speak before the last person in line walked onto the bus. The driver looked forward and sighed, allowing a few more moments to pass before he closed the door. Jenica jumped onto the bus and watched Mircea wave goodbye from the sidewalk.

What a surprise, he thought as he peered into the envelope to make sure the tickets were genuine. As the bus drove down the street, he started thinking about how much his girlfriend, Virginia, would love these tickets.

Virginia was studying to become a doctor. She was a beautiful woman inside and out with long black hair which touched her hips and big brown eyes. Each day, Jenica was amazed at her quiet strength. When they were out together, Jenica felt proud each time he was next to her. Unable to hide the flood of emotion in his face, he remembered Mircea's last words.

"Jenica, not a word to Virginia, OK? I'm sorry to add stipulations like this, but the tickets have to look like they were your idea. Doina's orders."

It seemed unlikely that Virginia would believe such a thing. Born in Dragoesti, a tiny village from the northern region of Moldova, she was the youngest daughter of Alexandru Gemanar, a kindhearted Romanian Orthodox priest. Alexandru was fifty-three years old when Virginia came into the world. Having already raised seven boys, he'd lost his taste for harsh discipline and could not resist spoiling Virginia, who stole his heart from the first moment he saw her. Watching her father turning the pages of a bible or book of poems, the girl had learned to read herself by the time she was five years old and had proved an intensely serious lerner from her first day at school. She was assertive and morally courageous.

From their first dates, Jenica was impressed with her variety of knowledge. He often told Mircea how bright she was and how well they got along. Jenica had never been able to fool or surprise her, but if a pair of concert tickets lay in the balance, he agreed that it was at least worth trying. Jenica thought of Mircea's smug look a minute ago.

They'd met a year earlier when Jenica had decided that the University of Cluj was situated in a city that was too old and that the capital of Romania had more to offer. Mircea, a native of Moldova, was initially skeptical about befriending Jenica, who was originally from the region of Ardeal—as a matter of course, *ardelenii* didn't get along well with *moldovenii*—but over time, they earned each other's trust despite constantly making fun of their respective lands of origin.

Near the Faculty of Law, the bus stopped. Jenica stepped toward the exit and out onto the street. As it was already late on a Friday, he decided to call Virginia from a phone booth rather than visit her apartment in person.

"Hello. Is this Miss Gemanar?"

"Yes," a woman answered. Then she took a severe tone. "Very funny, Jenica. Now, what are you up to?"

"I was just wondering if you were busy this weekend."

"Maybe. Did you have something in mind?"

"I thought maybe we could go to a concert together at the Athenaeum?"

"Are you serious? I'd love to!"

"Great. I'll see you tomorrow morning at around ten thirty. We could meet in front of the statue of Mihai Eminescu."

"Our beloved poet?"

"That's the one. I'll see you then. And please, Virginia, try not to be late. If I'm a few minutes behind, just pass the time talking to the godfather."

"You want me to talk to a statue?"

"Not just any statue. He's the godfather of Romanian poetry."

Virginia braced herself for another sprawling lecture on Eminescu—or Nicolae Iorga, a historian and one of the poet's greatest admirers. But instead, she preemptively interrupted: "Of course, I almost forgot. I'll see you soon, Jenica."

In the year that she had been dating Jenica, the two had spoken quite a few times about seeing a concert together at this magnificent building situated in the city's central neighborhood. Still, their busy schedules always got in their way.

* * *

The sun had risen high by the time she woke up the next morning. She took a quick shower, put on her blue dress, and went into the kitchen for breakfast. She realized soon that she was not hungry, so she just made herself a cup of warm tea.

A few rays of the sun cut through the kitchen window of her small apartment. She closed her eyes and let them warm her face.

Oh, look at this beautiful day, Virginia thought, looking outside the window. *I think I may walk to the Athenaeum. If I cross Piata Palatului, I should be there right on time*, she reasoned, looking at the old cuckoo clock in the living room.

5

Yes, I think that's a good idea. Well, I better start walking if I don't want to be late. She grabbed her coat and purse, and headed out.

As soon as she started walking, she realized it was still cold. Virginia gave it another thought. *I should have taken the bus. Now it's way too late*, she worried. She started walking faster and faster. *I should have taken the bus.*

Right at that moment, she spotted them.

There, I can see them both—the building and the statue, just like Jenica told me.

She stopped for a minute to catch her breath. Virginia looked with admiration at the symphony of music and poetry unveiling in front of her: the Romanian Athenaeum, the George Enescu Philharmonic Orchestra hall (named after the famous Romanian composer), and the Mihai Eminescu statue.

Virginia checked her watch and exhaled with relief. It was ten thirty sharp, and by then, she was right in front of the green and gray bronze statue of Eminescu, looking around to see if, by any chance, Jenica was already there.

There is still plenty of time till the concert starts, she thought. Feeling sore calves from her brisk walk across the neighborhood, she sat on one of the benches near the statue to rest her legs. Virginia was excited and unable to keep still. She fiddled with a brooch Jenica had given her at Christmas: a tiny flower with straight, narrow petals that radiated from the center like the points of a star. Romanians call it *floare de colt*, an alpine flower symbolizing courage and rugged beauty. It was the first gift that Virginia received in a long time. That little flower that was once called *Floarea reginei* (the queen's flower) brought her so much joy that it became part of her daily wardrobe.

Looking up from the brooch, she noticed something about the statue she had never seen before. It wasn't apparent in the noontime light, but if you looked closely, you could see that Eminescu was sculpted undressed with just a thin loincloth around his waist.

Look at that body, she thought. Giggling and smiling, Virginia contemplated sharing her discovery with Jenica when he arrived for the concert. She again checked the time and saw that it was fifteen minutes to eleven. *Jenica will be here any minute now*, she thought.

She waited… and waited… and no sign of Jenica. Maybe he got stuck in traffic; it was not unusual for the buses to be late and overcrowded on a Saturday.

"Where is Jenica, Godfather?" She asked him with a quavering voice. *What if something unexpected happened to him?* she thought. Jenica was not always on time, but he was never fifteen minutes late on their dates. She again checked the time a saw that it was almost eleven. Virginia waited till the Athenaeum doors closed, then she slowly rose from the bench and walked to a phone booth across the street to call Jenica's dorm.

On Saturdays, Jenica's friend Mircea tended to roll out of bed at ten or eleven to prepare a traditional Romanian breakfast for his girlfriend, Doina, and himself. He had earned a reputation for making the perfect *mamaliga*—a porridge of boiled water, salt, and cornmeal, like the Italian polenta—and the essential items in a Romanian breakfast, including fried eggs, cheese, butter, and sour cream.

Virginia at first hesitated to call him. She knew that her roommate, Doina, was there, and she didn't want to be a bother. But after she called Jenica's dorm, she had a change of heart and dialed Mircea's number.

"Hi, Mircea. Is Jenica there by any chance?"

"I haven't seen him. I thought he was with you."

"We were supposed to meet in front of the Mihai Eminescu statue to go see a concert at the Athenaeum."

"Hmm, is that right? Well, maybe he overslept. Did you check at the dorm?"

"Yes, and they told me that they hadn't seen him this morning."

"That's weird. I think you should check at the library. That's the only place I can think of."

"OK, I'll go look for him there. Maybe he was studying and lost track of time."

"Virginia," Doina interrupted, grabbing Mircea's phone. "Why don't you come over for breakfast, and then we can all go together to look for him? I am sure nothing serious happened to him. You know how forgetful Jenica can be."

"I'd rather figure out where Jenica's ended up, and I am just a few minutes away from Piata Palatului from where I'm calling."

"Can we meet you at the library in about twenty minutes? We'd like to help," Mircea insisted. Virginia could hear the worry he was trying to conceal from her.

"Fine, I'll see you at the library," Virginia said, sighing as she hung up the phone.

With its bronze outdoor statue of Carol I and its facade of limestone molding and columns, the Central University Library was an impressive building. Its stacks contained over half a million books. The silence walking inside the atrium could feel like entering a church, as it was capped by an immense dome of polished marble and chandeliers and surrounded by dozens of wood-paneled reading rooms where students sat for hours at a time.

Jenica was an insatiable reader, and it wasn't unusual to find him there, running his finger over a page or grinning as his pen scratched against a sheet of notebook paper. But this time, he was nowhere to be found.

Having checked each study room twice, Doina and Mircea shrugged their shoulders as they crossed paths with Virginia in the main hallway. "I don't think he's here. We've looked everywhere," Mircea said. He had even looked through the restroom and craned his neck under the stall walls to see if he recognized Jenica's reddish-brown leather shoes.

"We were supposed to all meet for lunch today, or that's what his intentions were yesterday. He wanted to surprise you both; he kept it a secret," said Virginia.

"Aha, then let's go back to my apartment and wait for him. You both go ahead. I'll stop to get a pack of cigarettes on the way home."

When they returned to Mircea's building, no one was waiting at the entrance. Nor had anyone used the key Mircea kept under his doormat to let himself inside. As they walked through the door and looked in the kitchen and living room, Virginia's sense of annoyance shifted to something closer to dread.

They waited and waited, with no sign from Jenica. Around noon, Mircea opened a bottle of red wine and arranged a small plate with aperitif containing a variety of traditional Romanian products made from a pig: caltabos, sangerete, and leber.

"Virginia, you must try the caltabos. It is so good. Doina almost ate it all yesterday," he told her.

"Do you have pork rind?"

"Of course, I do. I kept some just for you. Jenica told me how much you like it."

He realized that he had just mentioned Jenica's name. Virginia looked at her watch. A few hours had passed since their date at the Athenaeum and no sign from Jenica.

"I need to go. I have to find Jenica." She got up from the table and started walking toward the door. Doina jumped up and grabbed her shoulder, trying to distract her.

"Let's wait for him here. He will be surprised to see us all waiting for him. We can surprise him with some *mititei*." Doina continued trying to persuade Virginia to stay by explaining that Mircea had learned how to make the Romanian sausage by following Jenica's aunt's recipe."

She eventually was able to detain her. Virginia tried hard to believe that there was a chance Jenica might walk through the door any minute, looking just as exasperated as his friends and apologizing to all of them.

Every few minutes, they would hear the street door open, and the floorboards creak beneath the stairs, but the apartment door never opened, and the doorbell never rang.

They listened to jazz music and drank more wine to soothe their nerves. Mircea tried to pat Virginia on the back and reassure her that nothing terrible had happened to Jenica, but by nightfall, he'd lost his sense of humor, too.

"Maybe we should call Jenica's aunt Oara. She'll want to know what's going on. Who knows, maybe Jenica went to see them yesterday and decided to spend the night at their house," Virginia told them.

Mircea shook his head. "Jenica never spent a night at their house since he moved to Bucharest, and at this hour, it'd be his uncle Aurel who'd answer the phone. He'll only gripe that we bothered him on a Saturday. Or he'll get angry and assume his nephew is in some kind of trouble. Jenica's aunt and uncle are party members—asking them about their nephew could do more harm than good. Aurel and Jenica used to argue a lot about politics until one day when Oara forbid them to talk about it. After all, they are supposed to report everything they see to the Securitate (the new name for the secret police)."

"If that's the case, then calling his family is definitely out."

"But what if Jenica is in trouble?" Doina wondered aloud. "Maybe he got involved with a dangerous crowd? Was he involved in any subversive activities or clubs? Maybe he was just a victim of circumstances: he got robbed on his way to meet Virginia or, worse, stabbed and killed. He could have been wandering home from some place drunk and gotten into a fight?"

Virginia shook her head. "None of those sound like Jenica; they're too out of character."

"You're probably right," Doina tried to agree. "Where is he then? What happened to him? I've only ever seen him here or in the library or maybe visiting his professors. It's not as if he's picked up some new hobby we don't know about, like gambling, or fallen in with some agitators who all meet in secret."

"What about the police?" Doina said, looking at Mircea.

"That's even more dangerous. Even if Jenica hasn't done anything wrong, there's no way we can look for him without drawing suspicion, and you all know that the police are working hand in hand with the Securitate. It could do more harm than good."

The three friends silently looked at each other, then down to the floor, as if buckling under a heavy weight. Virginia felt a cold draft enter the room.

"If I don't hear from him tonight, first thing tomorrow, I'll go check his dormitory and go through his belongings, papers, diaries, et cetera. Anything to find clues."

"That's a good idea," Mircea agreed. "But remember, no one can know we're looking for Jenica. Then again, we don't even know for sure that he's missing. If you run into any students, tell them Jenica's mother fell suddenly ill, and he had to go to see her immediately. I'll do the same, and I'll see what I can find from my cousin Dinu."

"The one who works at the Ministry of Public Safety?" Virginia asked. "Isn't he a Party member?"

"I know. I know," Mircea said. "I'll have to be very careful. But we need to find out if there have been any reports of muggings, robberies, or murders in the area that might somehow indicate that Jenica was involved. So that's the plan for now. We will quietly investigate the presumed disappearance without telling anyone. We will look for anything to find clues."

Exhausted and full of nerves, Virginia stood up and began to put on her coat. Doina walked her to the door, rubbing her shoulders a few minutes before kissing her on the cheek.

"I'll talk to Jenica's roommate, Eugene; I suppose it might be useless—that boy is so absentminded. But it's worth a shot, right?"

Before she left, Virginia added, "Wish me luck. I'll be back here at four o'clock to hear what you've found." She could hear the door lock behind her as she walked down the stairs.

Back at her apartment, she tried for hours to fall asleep. Jenica's unexpected disappearance kept her awake and wondering. What happened to him? The question so tormented her that she started thinking the worst, even the possibility that he might have been abducted and killed and that she would never see him again.

No, Jenica is not dead. I will find him. When she finally closed her eyes, it was almost three in the morning.

Chapter Two

B esides being one of the oldest dormitories at the university, with brass window fittings and stone floors that were impossible to keep clean, Jenica's residence had the highest concentration of students. In the morning, the sidewalk was full of half-asleep students rushing to their lectures, munching apples, and tucking in their shirts. The front door was nearly blocked off in the afternoon by huddles of young men smoking, gossiping, and exchanging boorish taunts.

Inside, a middle-aged security guard sat in the atrium, tugging at his mustache and flipping through a paperback. Though his post required vigilant attention to ladies attempting to visit in the evening, he often paused from his shift in the late afternoons for a nap at his desk. Besides, few female students ever ventured into the hallways. The lights were always on, the noise never seemed to cease, and the smell of unwashed laundry never seemed to dissipate.

While walking up to the fifth floor, Virginia heard a familiar voice and saw Jenica's ex-roommate Luca. She noticed a red and swollen spot over his left eye.

"Have you been walking into streetlamps?"

Luca gave her a quizzical look.

"Oh, you mean this," he said, moving a finger over his temple. "Yup. That's just what happened. I've been so tired in the mornings that I run to class without watching where I'm going."

"You should be more careful. Does it still hurt?"

"Maybe just a little," he answered, as if unsure of what to say. "What brings you to the fifth floor?"

"Jenica asked me to bring back some study material that he left at my house."

"Oh, I see."

"Have you seen Jenica this morning?"

"I did this morning coming out of the library," said Luca, momentarily looking at the floor. The bruise did look painful.

Belying her true feelings, Virginia looked calmly at her watch and saw it was almost one o'clock.

"I think I'll wait for him to get home."

Luca quickly said, "I overheard Jenica saying something about going somewhere after finishing his study and not to expect him back…"

Virginia finished Luca's sentence: "Expect him back…anytime soon, you mean."

Luca's stack of books appeared to be coming apart, and he hiked them back toward his chest. He quickly corrected himself, "I mean, you *should* expect him back. Sorry. I mean, he'll turn up again soon."

"No, I got it," Virginia tried smiling to conceal her nerves. She thanked him and watched as Luca nodded and paced over to the stairwell. She knocked at the door, waited a minute, then opened Jenica's door. Eugene was not in the room.

She looked around. Compared with other dorm rooms, Jenica's room was tidy. There were no dirty socks on the floor, the trash bin was empty, and blankets and sheets lay neatly over the bed. Virginia picked up a brushed-silver frame above Jenica's desk, housing a photograph he'd taken of her during a trip to the mountains. Although the shelf was dusty, the rest of the desk looked like it had just been wiped without any notebooks or scribbled pieces of paper strews. The bookshelf, Virginia thought, was not tidy as usual, and it looked like quite a few books were missing. She laid the study material on Jenica's desk and sighed. What happened with Jenica's books? Virginia tried to open his closet, was locked. She looked under his bed and found a big suitcase. When she opened it, the pungent smell of mold made her sneeze. She did manage to look inside and saw a lot of scrape books. She checked one more time each drawer of the desk. There didn't seem to be anything of interest. She looked at her watch and gasped; it was getting late. She again looked around one more time before she rushed out the door.

* * *

Doina convinced Virginia to let her talk first with Jenica's roommate, Eugene.

"Maybe he knows some of Jenica's secrets, and he might feel uncomfortable sharing them with you. Maybe he's involved with another girl—it's not unusual for boys his age."

"I don't think so. Jenica is more involved with schooling than girls," countered Virginia with a wry scowl.

"OK, all I am trying to say is that we need to think outside the box."

"OK, Doina, if you say so. Eugene might be out of town. Wait till Monday to go and talk with him," Virginia suggested.

Mircea gave Doina precise instructions on where to find Eugene. She could hear a bell from the next street over. Then, a line of students spilled out into the atrium of the law building. Jenica's roommate was the last to leave. He patted his pockets for cigarettes and matches. When he finally drew a puff of smoke, he saw Doina waving at him.

"How goes it?" he asked, giving a cheerful bow.

"I'm doing fine. I was wondering if you have seen Jenica lately?"

Eugene looked confused. "No, not since Friday anyway. What's up? Is anything wrong?"

"Not at all. It's just that Mircea is trying to track him down. Next weekend, we want to set up a trip to Mogosoaia, but it feels like herding cats. Men are terrible at organizing."

"All right then," Eugene said, looking down, smiling. "I saw an envelope on Jenica's desk the other day, and when I opened it, there were two tickets to a concert at the Athenaeum." Eugene was ready to leave when he turned around and told her, "I think you should check with his girlfriend, Virginia. I am quite sure he went to the concert with Virginia."

He smiled again and saluted with two fingers as he walked across the street. Doina looked over her shoulder and walked down the road to meet Virginia.

"That was Eugene, right?" Virginia questioned her, taking a sip from a cup of tea.

"Yes, he told me that he hasn't seen Jenica since Friday and that I should check with you. He saw the concert tickets on Jenica's desk."

Virginia sighed and shook her head. "I want to look in Jenica's room one more time, but, honestly, there wasn't anything to see. The only thing that bothered me was Luca's demeanor. The whole time he avoided eye contact. Then his responses were quick and vague. He tried to rush off not to have to answer more questions. And he had a big swollen spot on one of his eyes."

"Maybe he went to the pub and started talking trash?"

"He says he walked into a streetlamp. I don't believe that any more than you do."

Doina looked at her watch. "Let's wait until the afternoon when we're sure they're out of the building. Then we'll give the room one more look. I can come with you."

"No, I'll go by myself." Virginia looked down, trying to hide her tears.

"Come on." Doina tugged her wrist. "We've got to keep at it."

Chapter Three

Sitting in the kitchen, Mircea swept a lock of hair away from his eyes and took a pull from a half-finished cigarette. He was studying for an exam on eighteenth-century philosophy for his master's degree. The text's vocabulary was OK and certainly more varied than what he'd read before university, but the material was dispiritingly thin. Between a few valuable bits on Costin, Conta, Maiorescu, Hasdeu, the book had page after page of frothy Party analysis: Stalin, Dej, and more Stalin. Mircea exhaled the last of his cigarette through his nose and snuffed out the end; then, he stood up to close the window. He'd pushed away his textbook and begun shuffling back through his lecture notes when he heard a knock on the door.

Virginia looked as he'd expected she would—pale and frazzled, with a coat draped clumsily over her shoulders. Doina looked somehow even more drained and sat at the table before he could clear space or offer her something to drink. He stood up chivalrously to offer Virginia a seat next to his own and then described his conversation with Dinu.

"It was frustrating," he explained, pulling some scattered notes into a neat stack. "Dinu's friends in the police are pretty green and relatively low rank. They have no access to the sections in charge of state security or anything related to political investigations. From all the reports, I decided that only three are worth inquiring about."

Mircea then got Virginia's attention.

"The first of these took place near the dormitory. Shortly before midnight on Saturday, a group of students at the pub got into a noisy argument and were asked to leave. The scuffle continued out in the street and did not subside until the management called the police. Four men were arrested, two of whom fit Jenica's description."

"What? No, this one is out of the question." Doina looked toward Virginia.

Mircea continued, "I agree that it sounds too frivolous for Jenica, but the second case is even less likely. Earlier in the evening, a pair of young individuals attempted to rob a stationery store near the East Station. One guy's description was similar to Jenica's."

Doina lost her temper and hissed at Mircea, "This is idiotic. All Dinu shared with you are two dead ends. Couldn't you at least get a name or two?"

"The third report," Mircea continued talking, "contains a young man found dead, facedown in an industrial district. Doina, you asked me about names? I'm sure you're aware this is forbidden knowledge for a civilian. Even asking about it can sound suspicious. Dinu had every reason to clam up, but I got him to talk. With any luck, he'll be visiting the morgue in a day or two."

Virginia's face was still blank, and she hadn't taken off her coat. Using a friendlier tone than Doina's, she said, "I appreciate your efforts. When are you meeting with Dinu next?"

"He agreed to have a mug of beer with me before the weekend. I'll ask if he can look into the reports and find out the identity of the murder victim. If he can shed any light on what's happened to Jenica, then I'm sure I can get it out of him. Dinu's a loyal functionary with a stable job, but three years without a promotion have made him resent his supervisor. I can't help but wonder if helping a guy like me doesn't give him a small thrill. We caught him at a good time. You might even say we're lucky."

"Sure," Doina commented. "Nothing but one good break after another."

"Doina—" Mircea wanted to argue with her, but Virginia stopped him.

"Let's keep it calm and avoid arguing with each other. I appreciate all the work you guys are doing to find Jenica. I think you both understand that the first two scenarios are out of the question. They are too out of Jenica's character. We are left with the third option. We need to find out who is that young man killed in the industrial area. Mircea, I count on you for that." Before she left, they all agreed to meet back at Mircea's place on Saturday.

* * *

On Friday, Mircea sat in the back of the crowded pub Carul cu Bere in a cobblestoned section of the student district. The bar looked crowded, but Mircea managed to find a table far away from the noise.

He looked at his watch. Dinu was late again. Right at that moment, he saw his cousin walking over from the other end of the block, wearing a gray wool coat that looked two sizes too big and keeping his head down as if studying the pavement in a trance. He'd been expecting Dinu to draw him into an entire evening of cheerful banter and jokes, but the young man in front of him hardly responded when Mircea stood up to wave and forced a smile.

"Have you got any cigarettes?" Dinu asked without saying hello. Before Mircea could reach for his pack and lighter, he stood up to order a coffee. He excused himself and went to the restroom.

"How is everything going at your job?" Mircea asked when he returned.

"You remember Lucian Vacarescu?" Dinu asked. "The guy from Suceava?"

"Two years ahead of us?"

"That's the one. And you know Monica Sturza? The tall, blue-eyed girl who looks like the Princess of Monaco? They're engaged now. Every Friday after her lectures finish, he puts on a crisp linen suit and takes her out on his motorbike. Then they have dinner in some Party functionary's house to drink whiskey and have fun. Of course, none of this ever made any sense to me. When he graduated, I'd always thought it was odd that he went to work for the Bank for Agriculture and Food Industry since loans and finances weren't his things, and I don't think he's ever seen a farm except through the window of a train."

He gulped up half of the beer mug and then crumpled into his chair and tilted back his neck as if it were unable to bear the weight of his head.

"Yesterday, I found out he'd been promoted again and heard someone snickering about it. Can you believe that? He is going to spend the next twenty-five years at an empty desk accepting bribes and picking his teeth and sleeping every night in a five-bedroom palace."

Mircea shrugged his shoulders and pouted his lips. "What's so upsetting about that?"

"Guess who he has promoted ahead of," Dinu said with a mean scowl. "It's never bothered me before to hear about some mediocre jerk getting ahead, but somehow I heard this business about Lucian, and now all I want to do is drink. No one in my family has taken a bribe in fifty years. It'll be a miracle if I ever move out of my parents' house. And I swear, the earth will crash into the sun before I have a motorbike, with or without a pretty fiancée on the back seat."

For a moment, it seemed as if Dinu had run out of breath. He emptied the other half of his mug with beer and leaned back again in his chair.

"I'm done, to be honest," he said. "I don't remember what this meeting was supposed to be. The homicide? Was that it?"

"Yes. Dinu, can you go to the morgue and see if there has been an update on the victim report about the identity of the murder victim?"

"I'll be blunt. I've tried five or six times over the past few days, except for today, of course. The only way I could even see the front door of the morgue was by quickly pacing by. Pretty soon, they're going to recognize my face."

"How hard would it be to see a copy of the report?"

Dinu refilled his coffee cup with rum and gave a skeptical look. "Wow. I guess it wasn't enough for me to stick my neck out just once, huh? You want me to keep pushing until I'm locked up in a labor camp?"

"None of the other leads have borne fruit. This homicide is a stretch, but I have to find out everything I can."

"The coroner's report is probably complete by now," Dinu said, "filed away with everything else. We'd have to look for it in the detective bureau."

"Jenica is my friend. And Virginia is counting on me. I don't care if we have to sneak in."

Dinu and Mircea stared at each other.

"Are you serious?" said Dinu. "You know how dangerous it can be?"

"Yes, I know."

Dinu was shocked. "You will risk your freedom–your life–for this guy? If I was in his place, would you risk the same for me?"

Mircea stared at him speechless. Dinu excused himself and went to the restroom. When Mircea tried to reopen the conversation, Dinu cut him off, raising his voice.

"With all due respect, why should I be helping you? You're going to flatter me into thinking we're friends? What do I have to gain? How, exactly, does this benefit my position?"

"You mean at the Party? That's a fair point," Mircea said. "I suppose I'd ask what those clowns have ever done for you."

For the first time, Dinu appeared to smile. "Maybe I'd resist more if I had the willpower," he said. "But I'm too exhausted. I guess we'll give it a try. Shame on you for catching me off guard like this."

Chapter Four

Since Jenica's disappearance, Virginia had neglected her studies. She could not concentrate and decided to take a leave of absence at the university. Nobody at the faculty asked her any questions. She had earned a reputation as an eminent student among her colleagues and professors. Virginia's family life was full of tragedy, and most of them were aware of it and offered to help her if they could—especially her anatomy professor.

"Virginia, is there anything that you need help with?"

"That's very kind of you to ask, but I can manage my affairs. I do appreciate your offer to help."

She rushed out of the faculty building before anybody else could ask her more questions. Walking down the street, she recalled the anatomy professor's last words: "By the way, Virginia, I've heard that the Romanian government is in final negotiations with the American government to buy the polio vaccine. Isn't that great?"

"Yes, sir," she answered and rushed out the door. She stopped near a store to catch her breath. Memories of her brother laying on the bed helpless started bothering her.

* * *

When Virginia crossed the street from the law building to the front of Jenica's dorm, it was almost five o'clock in the afternoon. She noticed a man sitting in the lobby but kept walking. As she passed the security guard's desk, she kept the hood of her mackintosh up so that it covered her ears, and she looked down at her watch.

Passing Luca's room, Virginia recalled his sinister smile and his eyes—the eyes of a hunter waiting in a field for the next victim. There was no way to tell if he knew anything about Jenica's disappearance. She started walking faster toward Jenica's dormitory, opened the door, and closed it quickly behind her. Her heart was pounding, and a strange feeling took over her body.

Jenica, where are you? She glanced around and noticed that Jenica's shelf had been cleared of books even more than when she was there. She tried to remember what books were missing but was unable to focus. *What is going on?* she wondered. *Jenica, where are you?* Virginia spun around and covered her face with both hands. Right at that moment, she recalled Jenica's face reading from a book written by historian Nicolae Iorga banned by the government called *Opinions sincères. Yes, that's the name.* Although it was a crime for any shop or printer to share a book by Iorga, he was Jenica's favorite author. She searched his desk but didn't find it. She looked under his bed and found a notebook hidden behind the books in his suitcase. Some pages from the notebook were torn out. She hastily looked through it, then hid it under her mackintosh. She heard people talking in the hallway. "*I have to get out of here. Something is not right,*" she thought and rushed to close the suitcase. She was almost ready to get out of the room when an intriguing conversation in the hallway between two students got her attention. As she listened to what they were saying, her face turned white, and her body started to shake. She held tight Jenica's notebook under her mackintosh, waited till the hallway was clear of voices, then rushed down the stairs to meet Doina. When she passed through the hallway, she bumped into a man. While apologizing, she glanced at him. He was the same man who she'd seen earlier in the lobby.

Out on the street, she started running, talking loudly, getting people's attention. "No, go away. You are not going to take Jenica with you." She ran, yelling hysterically.

Doina saw Virginia exiting the dorm; she was unsure of what happened when she saw her running. She got scared but decided to follow Virginia, ensuring nobody was following her.

"Virginia, Virginia, wait." Doina tried to get her attention. Finally, she grabbed her by the mackintosh and restrained her. Virginia looked at her, totally absent.

"Virginia, what is going on? Talk with me, please," Doina pleaded with her.

Virginia was unresponsive.

"Let's go home," Doina suggested. Looking at Virginia, she changed her mind and encouraged her to go inside a cafe nearby, and helped her sit at one of the tables.

Doina gave her some time to recover, then in a lower pitch and looking around to see if nobody was watching, she asked her again what happened.

"I overheard a discussion about a raid the Securitate did at the dorm not long ago," Virginia finally told her.

They were both aware that since the student movement a year ago against the government, the Securitate started popping out unexpectedly at the students' dorms to look for suspicious activities. Rumors circulated through the country's campuses that the Securitate increased the number of recruited students and professors to work for them. In exchange, they were offered tickets to festivals, promotions, or good-paying jobs in big cities. While some agreed to work for them, others were afraid to work for those disheartened individuals.

"What if the Securitate took Jenica?" Virginia told her in broken speech.

"Arrested him? For what reason? I know Jenica is not a fan of the regime, but they have to have a reason to do that."

Virginia looked down to the floor and said nothing for a while. Then, with a shaking voice, she told Doina, "It's not unusual for those monsters to come and pick up students for interrogations for whatever reason. Last year, when I was volunteering at the Cantacusino hospital, I witnessed a raid done by the Securitate at the hospital one day during the student revolt. Their agents came and picked up some injured patients, and nobody could stop them. I thought of what might have happened to them. They were probably thrown in jail or, worse, killed. They were wounded patients, Doina!" Virginia searched her purse for a handkerchief. Her entire body trembled as she tried to rid herself of the idea that the Securitate took Jenica.

"Jenica…Jenica…" she continuously called his name through tears.

Doina tried to distract her. "Virginia, why don't we go home? It is getting crowded here."

While she was talking, Doina noticed that Virginia was absentminded. "Virginia?" Doina touched her hand. "Virginia, are you OK? If you prefer, we can go to Mircea's apartment."

Virginia looked pale. She tried to get up from her chair and almost lost her balance. Jenica's notebook that she hid under her mackintosh fell to the ground. Doina rushed to pick it up.

"I am OK. I'd rather go to our apartment," said Virginia, then grabbed the notebook from her hands.

Doina looked at her and shook her head. "I'll come with you. I'll call Mircea later and let him know that we are together."

Hanging on each other they strolled towards the bus station and back safely to their apartment. Doina helped her lay down. Virginia grabbed her by the wrist. "Thank you for everything," she told her gratefully.

Doina smile, "I know you will do the same for me." She strengthen her blanket then got up from the bed and went to call Mircea.

She looked through the door at Virginia, who was sleeping. *Poor Virginia.* Doina took a deep breath, then let it out. Her mind went back in time and recalled the day she saw Virginia with Jenica for the first time.

She and Mircea planned it all out. They introduce them to each other.

Sitting at the table in Mircea's apartment, Jenica wore a new white shirt that still showed creases from the packaging. His eye contact was unsteady. He had put on aftershave, and the smell had overwhelmed Virginia from across the room. The attraction was by no means instantaneous. That night, Jenica talked a lot about books that he'd read or pieces of music he'd listened to that no one else had heard of. While he was talking, Doina noticed his devotion to a small handful of the obscure authors seemed almost maniacal. Jenica struck her as awkward and not entirely comfortable in his skin, but he was "bright and full of energy and passion, with a gentle voice and a disarming smile." That's how Virginia described him on their first date in the Cismigiu Gardens. Virginia told her that Jenica was more relaxed the second time they met and managed half a dozen times to make Virginia laugh. Jenica recited Virginia from Eminescu's poems, and she was delighted. There was no better place to listen to Jenica than near Eminescu's spring in Cismigiu Gardens. The area had become one of their favorites. Though Jenica was a daydreamer, Doina thought he was courteous. Virginia told her once that, although she couldn't always tell where his mind had wandered to, Jenica had an authentic and vigorously sincere way of speaking that made her feel grounded and secure. For the first time since losing her father and brother, Virginia had started believing she could restore a sense of fulfillment and inner peace. She was learning how to live again and feeling her feet tread steadily on the ground beneath her. But now, Jenica was missing.

* * *

Mircea rushed to enter the apartment carrying a big bag with food. His cheeks were red, and his coat was wet. Doina jumped from the couch and helped him take the bags in the kitchen. Mircea wrapped his arms around her. The sweet smell of her body enveloped him. He kissed her neck lightly then kissed her on the mouth hungrily.

Chapter Five

M ircea wondered if he'd gotten the dates wrong. The aluminum file cabinet was rusty and marked with hundreds of minor dents, and there were deposits of lint in the rails of each drawer, but the contents themselves looked altogether fresh and orderly. Each month of the year had its own section. A colored tab separated each week, and each day had its folder with thirty or forty sheets of crisp paper inside. Mircea guessed there was a loose rack or tabulator on whatever typewriter the reports were written on since the lowercase *m*'s and *n*'s were out of line with the other letters, but everything was still perfectly legible. What's more, he recognized many of the crimes, which were described in a short paragraph at the top of each first page: a burglary four blocks from the mathematics building, vandalism near the library, and an act of arson in an apartment building near the edge of town, in addition to the robbery and football scuffle Dinu had told him about.

"Did you forget your glasses?" he heard Dinu hiss.

"I can read everything fine."

"Then what's taking so long? I need to take a leak."

Dinu had a lot of energy for a guy who'd been steadily drinking beer all afternoon and evening. After they'd met outside the same pub in the cobblestone district as they had the day before, he'd walked ahead of Mircea across the streets and to the alley behind the detective bureau, like a young Labrador on a hunt. There'd been a sharp, purposeful look in his eyes when he peered over both shoulders and walked up to the back door. He leaned into the doorjamb with an impressive delicacy and turned an old and decaying brass knob without a key. The hallways inside had just a trickle of streetlight, and only when Dinu had stopped moving had the wobble in his posture become noticeable.

He'd indicated the archives room by jerking his head to the left, and he said something about standing just inside the door that led out into the alley. Mircea knew he would have to move quickly, and it took less than half a minute to find the folders containing the previous week's reports, but soon enough, he began to wonder if the sound of his heartbeat was audible out in the street. Finally, he paced furiously to the door and started to whisper.

"You'll have to look too," he told Dinu. "For the life of me, I can't find the report with anything like the homicide you described."

Dinu sighed.

They switched places, and for another two minutes, Mircea could hear a rapid shuffling of papers and file folders. The opening and closing of the aluminum drawers were interspersed with long silences and whistles of air through Dinu's nostrils. When Dinu walked back toward the door, nothing was in his hands. The lights turned on unexpectedly in the hallway, and he could hear men's voices. He signaled to Mircea to be quiet. Through the window, he could see men in leather coats. Mircea tried to keep calm. He began to sweat profusely. They stayed still till the men turned the lights off and left the building.

"Who were they?" Mircea rushed to ask him.

"For sure, the Securitate. Who else on earth would come here at this time of day?" he told him, frustrated.

"We've got to get going," Dinu said, and in another moment, they were out in the street. "I would have doubted it if I were looking alone, but we're both pretty bright guys, aren't we? The file isn't there."

"You mean it's filed in some other part of the station? We were look-ing in the wrong place?" Large sweat droplets dotted Mircea's forehead. Under the streetlamp, he saw that Dinu's face was more flushed than it had been at the pub.

"We were looking in exactly the right place," Dinu said, refusing to break his stride until they'd walked an entire two blocks. "I checked the weekly master lists to be certain. The homicide isn't there either. I sup-pose one explanation is that we're both hallucinating, and the homicide never happened…or more likely, the Securitate had taken an interest in the incident and had erased the report to clear their tracks. Which option would you prefer?" And with that sobering question, Dinu ended their conversation.

* * *

Early the following day, Mircea stopped at Virginia's apartment to help her absorb the news of the missing report. When she opened the door, the young woman's stomach was already a ball of cramped knots. Still, she began to feel especially weak when Mircea explained what had happened at the detective's office. Once he shared Dinu's interpretation that the ho-micide report had been scrubbed from the records, Virginia began to sense the strong possibility that the Securitate was watching the case. At that moment, it felt as though the blood were rushing out of her body. She tried to brace herself on the edge of a high coffee table. But her grip wasn't firm enough, and she lost her balance. After silently shuddering and writhing on the floor with her mouth open, she let out an angry scream. Mircea rushed to help her. She refused his help, furious.

"Mircea, how is it possible for a report to vanish after less than a week? I don't understand how a murder report can no longer exist in any list. We have to find the identity of the body. Is there any way?" she told him, angry and frustrated.

"Virginia, you should try to talk with Jenica's uncle Aurel. Maybe you can tell him the truth, that Jenica is missing, or maybe we can think of something without telling him the truth."

"I will go talk with Aurel and Oara, but I can't tell them the truth. I think I should wait and instead just tell them that my brother is missing, and I need Aurel's help to find him without police involvement."

* * *

When she heard the bell ringing in a nearby clock tower, Virginia realized a whole week had passed since her date at the Athenaeum on Saturday morning. The eleven iron tolls were unfamiliar, and yet they were altogether soothing to hear as she walked through a block of ten-story flats in the Giurgiului quarter, looking for Jenica's uncle and aunt's address.

His aunt Oara answered the street buzzer in a deep and slightly nasal voice and smiled when she opened the door to the second-floor apartment. She wore a khaki apron over her skirt. His uncle Aurel was sitting on the sofa with his back to the window, flipping through the Party newspaper *Free Romania* and listening to the radio. He switched it off when Virginia entered the room.

He stood up and nodded. Then he raised his eyebrows upon seeing the look of dizziness in Virginia's eyes. Even though four hours had passed since her conversation with Mircea, and she'd had time to wash her face and put on fresh clothes, it was evident to Oara and Aurel that she could barely bear the weight of the purse slung over her shoulder. Not knowing her well, they were made slightly uncomfortable by the unexpected visit—even before they'd heard why she was there—and yet it only fitted that they should greet her politely and offer her a cup of tea.

"I'm so sorry to interrupt your Sunday like this...." Virginia started, holding the cup with both hands as she sat in a hardwood chair across from Aurel.

"Nonsense," he replied, unsmiling and tugging at the edges of his mustache. "What is the purpose of your visit?"

"My brother Eusebius recently transferred from Iasi and has studied here in Bucharest since the start of the year. He's a responsible young man, very serious—more mature than me, in fact—and has lived in this neighborhood in a tiny boardinghouse where he can study at home without being bothered by roommates. I rarely hear from him, but we recently had plans to attend a concert together, and he never showed. I called, but no one answered, and his landlady says she hasn't seen him."

"How long ago was the concert?" Oara asked.

Virginia thought about the bell tower.

"It's been a full week now," she said. "I'm close to telling our mother, but it seems prudent to try and turn over every stone before I make her worry."

"It surprises me," he said, "that you have waited this long without notifying the police. How long has he been living in the city? Does he know his way around? If you'd trusted the authorities and allowed them to do their work, perhaps they would know something by now."

"Some friends of Eusebius have asked around for me," Virginia said, and then she watched as Aurel and Oara's faces expressed varying looks of impatience. "It seems unlikely that he would have gotten into trouble—real trouble, I mean—but we've come across a homicide report in which the victim fits his description."

"A homicide report?" Oara stammered, looking toward the window and shaking her head. "I'm not even going to ask how you found such a thing."

Aurel nodded. "It certainly seems funny how you managed to access confidential information meant for law enforcement but couldn't be bothered to file a report of your own. That's the trouble with your generation, isn't it? Never willing to face a problem squarely, always trying to cut through the tangle instead of letting the grown-ups—"

At that moment, Virginia's eyes began to water.

"Instead of letting the grown-ups cut through the tangle for us?" she demanded. "Is that what grown-ups do? Is it? Should I expect an exhausted policeman to take my problem and handle it seriously—and not cut corners and be lazy, venal, and incompetent and lie right to my face?"

Aurel leaned back in his chair but nodded to Virginia, encouraging her to continue.

"You, of all people, should understand what I'm talking about," she said. "It's not going to hurt my little feelings if you look at the floor and say something surly about young people and breaking through the tangle. Honestly, go right ahead."

"You're expecting us to help? We barely know you," Oara said. "Aurel and I are members of the Communist Party. We attend meetings and write letters and serve on neighborhood committees."

"All I'm trying to do is find my brother. Frankly, I'm too tired to waste anyone's time, and my nerves are too frayed to risk ruining your peaceful afternoon. I have a tiny shred of information about a boy who was found facedown a few nights ago behind a warehouse near the end of the Sector Six bus line."

"What legitimate business would your brother even have in the industrial district?"

"None that I know. It's a long shot. I'll admit that from the start. But the victim fits my brother's age, height, and weight, and if I can only confirm his identity, then I'll at least be able to talk to my relatives back home and not sound like a fool, with no bearing, who can't manage to look after her closest sibling."

Aurel and Oara exchanged glances. Outside, the bell tower struck twelve times.

"I might be able to pull some strings and find out some information. One of my old friends, in army command, now works with the police," Aurel said. "If you'd like me to ask about his contacts in the detective bureau, then

I suppose I can oblige without ruffling too many feathers. Are you telling us the report was from the past week? Are there any other details?"

Virginia shook her head.

"Fine. I'll figure out a way to contact you if I find anything, but you mustn't come through this neighborhood until then. Understood? And certainly, don't try to call or write. You're a sweet girl, but I'm not about to show my hand and land myself on some Securitate watch list for a meaningless dead-end lead—or worse, the information I'm not supposed to have because it's none of my business."

"I appreciate you trying to help me out, sir. And know that I don't try to create any problems for you and your wife, especially knowing that you both are members of the Communist Party."

"Never mind that. You're skinnier than when I last saw you, and you've got bags under your eyes. Is it all because of this trouble with your brother?"

"I suppose so."

"Don't worry. I'll find someone who knows what's going on. But stay the hell away from here, OK? If my contacts can't come up with anything within ten days, then I'll let you know."

Before walking Virginia to the door, Oara grabbed from the kitchen a bag in which she packed a homemade cake with walnuts and raisins. "For you and Jenica. I baked it last night. How is he doing? Tell him to visit me and bring his Moldovan friend Mircea with him. That boy is so funny. Did he tell you that I taught him how to make mititei and sarmale in vine leaves?" Oara didn't wait for her to answer the question. She hugged her, kissed her on the cheek, and waved her goodbye.

When she was out on the street, the midday sun and the monotone paint on the building facade made it challenging to discern which direction she had arrived in. Virginia regained some of her bearings after reading a street sign at the corner, but for the first minute, she felt utterly lost.

Chapter Six

A whole week had passed since Virginia's conversation with Aurel and Oara. Then one day, she found a note in her mailbox.

* * *

Virginia drifted from one end of the park to the other, dragging her toes on the ground every few steps and peering down a row of elms to see if she recognized whoever was approaching from the other side of the street. It was getting dark. When the streetlights finally turned on, she rewound her scarf around her neck and pulled the ends of her jacket tightly around her waist. At just the moment she was going to look down the elm row for the fifth time, she recognized Aurel, walking in a slow and confident gait toward the park.

"I'm sorry for being late," he said and removed a pair of finely stitched suede gloves from his pocket. "It's hard to find a wide-open place without too much auto traffic and safe enough for people to walk through, without a lot of alleys and doorways."

"Why is that important?"

"It's easier to follow someone and still keep your distance if there's a corner you can duck into and hide. I suppose that wouldn't be a problem at a big roundabout, but I'd rather not get hit by a car," he said, carefully putting on the gloves. "I'm also sorry to have left such a cryptic note in your mailbox. I assume it was easy enough to decode—the initials A. and O., with the building across from the park as a return address?"

"I managed all right," she said and watched a bushy-haired terrier mix shuffle by, its leash held by a middle-aged woman who seemed to be making a special effort to look straight at the ground. The woman took something out of her inside pocket, and Virginia's pulse went up for a moment. But then the dog squatted, and she could see the woman clean up the mess with a small grocery bag.

"The boy they found in the, let's call it, 'industrial district' is named Adrian Bisu. Does that name mean anything to you?"

"No." Virginia breathed a sigh of relief. Aurel noticed right away.

"Not your brother?"

"No."

"And it's still possible that your brother was in the industrial district, late on a Saturday night?"

"Yes."

"And you still don't know where he is?"

"I…I've got no idea," Virginia stammered.

Aurel nodded and pouted his lips. Then he removed a small, folded piece of paper from his wallet.

"You may think you know what you're doing," he said. "But I doubt it."

After looking over both shoulders, he pushed the paper into Virginia's hand.

"This paper I found it on the victim's body. My guess is since he was already dead, the Securitate rushed the search and overlooked. We don't know the circumstances the victim died. Anyway, the writing on the paper looks like Jenica's, but I might be wrong. You didn't mention anything about Jenica. Is he doing all right? Tell him that Oara would like him to come to visit."

"I will tell him. He's busy with school right now."

Aurel looked her straight in the eyes. "That writing, though. I am sure that was Jenica's, but why was the paper in this individual's pocket? Maybe Jenica knew him. I hope not. Remind Jenica that Oara would like for him to come to visit us. We would like both of you to come to have dinner with us one night. Oara will cook cabbage rolls with polenta and sour cream—-Jenica's favorite dish. Virginia, I hope you find your brother. Take care of yourself." He saw the dark circles around Virginia's eyes. "Try to get some sleep."

Virginia could hear the terrier barking from the far end of the park. Her eyes welled with tears again.

"Thank you," she said and stuffed the paper into her glove. "And I will. Thank you. Thank you. Thank you."

"The student district is that way, yes?"

Virginia nodded. Aurel began walking in the opposite direction and turned back one last time to touch his eyebrow with two fingers in a faint salute.

After Aurel was far enough away, she looked at the paper and noticed that it was notebook paper and an edge was frayed, as if it had been ripped out of the notebook. She recognized Jenica's writing and started trembling. She looked again and noticed some strange markings: the sentence "Bring your Carpati cigarettes and remember a spark," a peculiar flower drawn with three circles as the center and eight petals, and "8.00."

Chapter Seven

"Who on earth is Adrian Bisu?" Mircea asked aloud.

None of them could say, but Jenica's handwriting on the note was unmistakable. It was difficult to rule out how they knew each other. How their relationship was connected, in turn, to the disappearance of the homicide report was an even more impossible riddle.

"I don't think we're going to get anywhere by just sitting here racking our brains," Virginia said. "It all feels like taking shots in the dark. Does anyone feel like going out for a bit? Something might pop up if we stroll through the neighborhood where Bisu's body was found."

Mircea snuffed out his cigarette, and Doina took her cup and saucer to the sink, swallowing the final gulp as she walked.

"Let's check the park first, and then we can cross the street and check the area where supposedly Bisu got killed," said Virginia.

* * *

Herastrau Park was full of children running around enjoying the cold fresh air. The harsh winter season took a toll on the park trees, depriving them of water and sunlight. They could see a pair of boaters lifting their canoe out of the water and wiping it down with wet cloths on a wooden rack. At one end of the meadow, a young girl with a rubber ball was playing fetch with her dog, and at the other end, a pair of teenagers sat on a bench, staring intently at each other and holding hands. Virginia smiled, looking at an empty chess table. During the summer, she and Jenica watched white-haired men in bow ties and tweed jackets playing chess at this tables installed near a row of park benches at the edge of the water. She recalled her long walks with Jenica through the park during the summer. After Cismigiu Gardens, Herastrau Park was their favorite place to spend their weekends. There was so much to do: walking through the park, enjoying a boat tour around the lake, eating and drinking at one of the many taverns, riding a bicycle, or going to visit the open-air Village Museum nearby. She could see the tallest buildings through the tree line, peeking up like the cornices of a medieval tower.

"It's getting dark. We gotta get going," Doina said, bringing Virginia back to reality.

"Yeah, let's go," Mircea told them and started walking back under the tree line that ran parallel to Soseaua Bucuresti-Ploiesti. Virginia remembered what Aurel had said about wide-open places where it was difficult to be followed and was ready to abandon the idea that Adrian Bisu could have been accosted anywhere near where they were standing. There was no reason a carefully planned ambush would take place in plain view of unsuspecting witnesses. Or perhaps Bisu's murder had been improvised, and the absence of witnesses was a lucky break for the attacker. Or maybe the entire business about a back alley had been an imprecise, vaguely credible detail that shouldn't have been taken literally.

They decided to dig deep and crossed the street again. They passed a grimy, half-empty tavern. Its front door was open, and a breeze picked up the scent of mildew and floor cleaner from inside. A loud radio played, and all the customers seemed to be men. Most were old and sat at tables closer to the sidewalk. However, Virginia could see a huddle of road builders seated in the back, talking excitedly and shouting orders at an exhausted older woman who stood behind the bar. Doina looked back after they'd walked another block and gave Virginia an exasperated look.

Virginia nodded and took a deep breath, enjoying a sense of relief as the noise faded behind them. They approached an expansive, neatly trimmed lawn facing the park, which bordered an even more expansive parking lot and a wide-open walkway covering three blocks of space. Behind it was the tallest building in the neighborhood, with half columns that ran between each row of severe, sharp-edged windows and a long needle that jutted up from the central facade.

"Look at this gigantic building," said Doina impressed.

"This is the House of the Spark," Mircea said, looking at the colosseum unveiling in front of him. "I don't know. I think I like better the city's old architecture, more influenced by the classical and French style."

It doesn't look anything like the Romanian architectural style, Virginia thought.

"Russians, they took over everything in this country, including the architecture," Mircea commented, looking at the Communist insignia of a hammer and sickle carved on the facade of the building, one among the many other Russian symbols that decorated the House of the Spark. Even though the building was impressive, it wasn't designed for the benefit of the Romanian people. Another trophy was built to bring grace to the Communist regime invented by Russians. All the Russian symbols were a testimony to the cause.

After passing a statue of Stalin, it was clear that Doina and Virginia were thinking the same thing. They all stopped, and Mircea patted a rhythm on the legs of his trousers.

He started, "Do you suppose the spark mentioned in the note—"

Doina shook her head. "Of course it was."

"We might not find the crime scene, but this was part of their code," said Virginia. "There's still no explanation I can think of for the number *8.00*, except for the obvious point that it could be a time. And what about the flower with eight petals? Maybe the petals have a meaning, or maybe they don't. That flower, though, looks familiar."

"I don't know. I don't have an answer yet," Virginia told them, looking at the death bed of flowers near the Stalin statue.

"I wonder if Jenica was supposed to meet Bisu that night," Mircea said. He paused and thought. "Behind the statue of Stalin. Who on earth chose this place anyway?"

"Yeah, that's weird—a gathering, possibly anticommunist, near Stalin's statue," said Doina.

"Or maybe it was a smart idea since no one would suspect they were meeting to discuss anticommunist subjects near a Communist dictator's statue," Virginia said. "Well, I think we saw enough for one day. Why don't we go home and try to warm up? My feet are starting to hurt worse than ever."

Spotting a bus coming, they started running toward the station. Virginia began complaining of a headache. A cold wind started to blow when they exited the bus. They all felt physically and mentally tired.

"It seems it's going to snow soon," Doina told them, looking at the sky and rubbing Virginia's back, encouraging her to walk.

Mircea made sure no one was following them and pulled the blinds closed as soon as they'd entered the apartment. They removed their coats and sat around the kitchen stove to warm up. Virginia even took off her shoes.

"Let's go over the facts one more time," Doina suggested. "A week ago, Bisu was alone, somewhere near the House of the Spark, carrying a coded message, almost certainly written by Jenica. It stands to reason that the disappearance of the homicide report was related to a gathering and that Jenica knew something about it. We can also assume that Jenica had some reason to hide his connection with Bisu, but the nature of that connection is still anybody's guess. It could have been illicit and perhaps illegal, possibly political, or perhaps merely private."

The other two nodded, and Doina took another breath. Mircea had a look of discomfort. "It's still possible that Bisu was given Jenica's message without knowing who Jenica was," he said. "For that matter, it's also possible that someone placed the note on Bisu person after he died."

"We could even imagine the missing homicide report having nothing to do with Jenica's vanishing," added Virginia. "But that's a very odd coincidence. If anyone had taken that file from the detective bureau, it would have been because the Securitate took an interest in the case. That implies Bisu was involved in some sort of—"

"Bisu could have been confused with someone else," Mircea said, looking down. "But Jenica is implicated. There's no mistaking that handwriting."

"I think they were planning a gathering behind Stalin's statue. And what would the gathering be about?" wondered Doina aloud. "What is this group that Jenica's involved with? And besides Bisu and Jenica, how many other people got involved? Forgive me if I'm getting ahead of myself, but we'll need to start talking to people as discreetly as we can to try to find more clues about what he was up to before he disappeared."

"You're right," Virginia said. "I guess I should go back to Jenica's room to find something that can help us crack the code."

"I'll handle that," Doina said. "Just tell me where to look. If Eugene and I cross paths, I'll be able to handle it. Maybe I'll even be able to read his expression and find out what he knows. Maybe he's not such a harmless philosophy guy after all, eh?"

Virginia was staring at Doina all this time. "Do you think he is trustworthy? What do you know about him?"

"I only saw him a few times. Mircea, you told me that Jenica likes him a lot. After his terrible experience with Luca being his roommate last year, he thought he was fortunate to find Eugene as a roommate."

"Yeah, that's right," Mircea agrees.

Doina continues talking. "If I had to describe him, I would say that he is timid and well-mannered but with terrible taste dressing himself—nothing in his appearance matches. I did notice that he likes to wear green and yellow a lot. I met him last spring at the Martisor festival at the university. Such a nice festival. Just like Jenica, Eugene was looking for a roommate."

Virginia looks towards Doina but says nothing. She got up from the chair and walked towards the window. She looked outside and thought back in time. Martisor, this authentic Romanian celebration, when Romanians celebrate the beginning of spring, was her brother Mitrita's favorite. Virginia smiled, recalling the little gifts that she used to get from him over the years as part of the tradition. Mitrita was very crafty and created simple but lovely gifts from flowers for her and their mother. As part of the tradition, men offered small little gifts to women to show their love and respect on that particular day, March 1. Virginia closed her eyes and thought, *Such precious memories*. A pat on her shoulder brought her back to reality.

"Don't worry, Virginia, I'll go talk with him tomorrow," Doina reassured her.

Chapter Eight

Eugene was in the room he shared with Jenica at five fifteen, leaning over his desk to study for an economics exam. Exhausted, he removed his glasses and rubbed the bridge of his nose.

"Don't lose your focus," he heard a voice say.

Startled, Eugene looked back toward the hallway and saw Doina leaning against the doorframe. Immediately he checked her out.

"How long have you been standing there?"

"Just for a moment."

"I was wondering if you knew some masterful strategies for staying alert and concentrating before an exam?" Eugene asked her, checking her out one more time.

"I wish. How are you doing? You look like you haven't got a care in the world."

"I've had a lot to deal with lately," Eugene told her.

"Then it's not a scholastic problem, huh?"

Doina shrugged her shoulders. She was ready to confide in Eugene, but not because she knew him particularly well or because he had any well-known talent for respecting the privacy of his friends. Jenica didn't know him that well either.

"I'm worried about Jenica," she finally said. "Virginia's having a tough time tracking him down. Have you noticed anything strange about him lately? When's the last time you two spoke?"

"I'm not sure," he said, allowing Doina to wonder if she sounded strange herself. "Though, now that I think about it, he did seem a bit concerned a few weeks ago. On the Friday before last, he wandered out of bed looking groggier than usual, went out to class, then came back to the dormitory looking jittery and ill at ease. He scribbled something in a notebook for a few minutes, and I thought maybe he was stressed about an exam. Then he went out again and stayed out until almost midnight."

"Hmm…it sounds strange," said Doina. "Maybe he was stressed about an exam. Eugene, would you mind if I looked for something else of Jenica's? It'll only take a minute."

Not at all, go ahead.

Doina ran her hands through the space between the desk and the wall and then opened each desk drawer, finding them empty. The bookcase was loosely packed. She flipped through the contents of every notebook to see if any others matched the paper found on Bisu's body. Finding nothing of interest, she ran the edge of her pinky behind all five rows of books and stopped when her hand hit something. At first, there were only a few thinner notepads that had been turned on their side, though she also found one or two pencil erasers and a small cardboard box of pen-ink cartridges, followed by an aluminum lighter and two packs of cigarettes.

Doina reeled back her hand, astonished. Everybody knew Jenica was not a smoker, yet the metal from the lighter had a dull shine from frequent use. Both packs had at least a few cigarettes missing. One brand was Snagov, with a red triangle on a white background, and the other brand was Carpati, showing the head and neck of an antlered stag on a green meadow.

"Are these yours?" she asked Eugene.

"No."

"Have you ever seen Jenica smoke?"

"No."

"It's quite impressive that he's kept this from us," she said, still trying to sound relaxed. "You'd think the habit would leave marks on his fingertips or at least some kind of odor on his clothes. The room doesn't smell bad at all."

Eugene was almost certain Doina meant this as a neutral compliment, but just to make sure, he discreetly sniffed an armpit stain he'd been trying to scrub out of his shirt. Then he attempted a smile while Doina settled the other books back into place.

"Interesting," she said. "Oh well. Do let me know if you see Jenica. Virginia wants to know where he's been."

"Sure, I added you to the list," said Eugene, annoyed.

Doina stopped and turned around. "What list?"

Eugene hesitated to answer.

"Eugene, what list are you talking about?"

"There are others who come and ask about Jenica."

"Who? Have you seen them before?"

"No, but one, in particular, told me he was a friend of Jenica's. His name was Tony. He told me to let him know if I saw Jenica. I got his phone number if you are interested."

"Sure, I would like to have it. Can you describe him?"

"Light blond hair and blue eyes. Very tall with a deep voice."

"Did he take anything that belongs to Jenica?"

"Oh yeah, he took a few books and notebooks from Jenica's desk. He told me that he desperately needed back the materials that Jenica borrowed from him."

Doina walked toward the door. "Eugene, if you do hear anything from Jenica, let me or Virginia know first, OK?"

Eugene nodded again and leaned back slightly in his chair, letting the book slide from the desk surface into his lap. Doina walked out of the room, tightly clutching the notebook that she took from Jenica's desk under her arm. After several attempts to read a single page of his study material, Eugene prepared to try again.

* * *

In Mircea's home, Doina showed him and Virginia the notebook and the cigarettes. They were all confused.

"If Jenica smoked in secret," Mircea said, leaning his elbows on the kitchen table, "I'd have thought we were close enough that he'd tell me."

Doina looked at him but said nothing.

For the past ten minutes, Virginia had been turning the pages of the notebook with surgical delicacy. She recognized notes about appointments for study groups and a few throwaway lines about dates when she and Jenica had eaten dinner or gone out to see a play, but filled in between were strange images of flowers and phrases that didn't make sense. "These are codes," Virginia thought while turning the pages.

"Look, Doina, all these passages are copied from the *Opinions sincères*. I've heard of messaging systems based on a random book, of which both sender and receiver have a copy," Virginia said. "You reference a recognizable page, and the other person looks it up to see what you mean. Perhaps the book itself is used for sharing messages in secret. But wait a minute. Isn't Iorga banned anyway?"

Mircea shakes his head in approval. "Absolutely. Especially after the protests last year. I can't say I'm not impressed that Jenica would have been bold enough to hold on to a book like this. It's one thing to listen to Radio Free Europe reports about resistance to Gomułka. Thousands of us listened to those. But a book is physical evidence. Simply possessing a copy could be dangerous, even if Jenica wasn't using it as a decoding text."

Doina folded her hair into a barrette and took a sip of the delicious wine that Mircea's father had brought. It slowly started sinking in that maybe Jenica was involved in a group behind the protests. "What was Jenica doing during those protests anyway?"

"We would have known," Mircea said, unsure of himself. "Maybe not right away. And maybe we would have doubted it at first, but I'm sure we would have figured it out eventually. I don't recall ever talking about the protests. There's simply no way Jenica could have been involved in an illegal political group and hid it from all three of us for more than a year. If he was involved, he hid it very well. Would it even be possible to hide his involvement so well from his closest friends?"

"I'm willing to set aside my hurt feelings for now," Virginia said, returning from the kitchen. "You should be too. It's all just speculation and rubbish unless we can figure out the code. To begin with, we've got to decide what those cigarettes were supposed to mean."

"Could they have been some special signal?" Doina suggested. "A sign of distress?"

"They could just be a red herring," Mircea cut in. "Sometimes, the most important part of understanding a cipher is separating the signal from the noise. Maybe Jenica was keeping the cigarettes for a friend. It's not unusual to have a pack of cigarettes around for guests."

"Why would he have two packs?" Doina asked.

"To make sure he has the brand his friends prefer," said Mircea. "Or perhaps he's selling cigarettes. If you know where to look and buy them in the right quantity, it's not a bad way to make extra money."

"Rubbish. Those kinds of cigarettes you can find everywhere. If they were Marlboro or Kent cigarettes, I might agree with you, but not Carpati or Snagov!"

"Virginia is right, Mircea. There are a thousand ways to make extra money and thousands of things that would be more practical for a student to sell. It isn't logical to imagine someone like Jenica transforming himself into a bourgeois salesperson out of nowhere. And besides, tracking down wholesale merchandise, even if it's legal, would take up all sorts of time and effort that he'd rather spend studying."

"He's developed some hobbies lately that we had no idea about," Virginia worried. "It could be that he's taken up tobacco. Or it could be that he's joined a clandestine anti-Stalinist action group trying to organize a student revolt. I'd like nothing more than for this story to be boring and silly and for Jenica to suddenly walk through our door and act surprised that we've gotten so upset, but the empirical facts point to something much nastier, and I don't know how we're supposed to—"

"Wait," Doina snapped, unfolding Bisu's note once more. "The note says, 'Bring your Carpati cigarettes and remember a spark.' He was counting on Bisu or someone else to know what that meant. Those cigarettes aren't meaningless. They aren't noisy. They were part of the code. Suppose we tried it ourselves? Could we carry them around visibly, maybe somewhere near Herastrau Park? Perhaps someone will approach us."

"Have you gone completely crazy?" Virginia said. "What if the Securitate is involved?"

"This is getting weird. I don't know about you all, but I need a break. Let's all go into the kitchen and eat something. Virginia, would you like some stuffed peppers with mamaliga?"

"I'll make some fresh mamaliga," said Mircea.

"We're at a dead end," Virginia continued while they all transited to the kitchen. "We can't be put off by the theoretical risks of showing our hand. I don't suppose it makes sense to walk up to random strangers on the street and ask how they feel about Jenica, Iorga, Carpati cigarettes, or the House of the Spark. Still, we haven't come across a single piece of valuable information so far without taking a chance. I doubt that's going to change."

"What about Jenica's other classmates?" Mircea asked. "Would it make sense to let them in?"

"Luca gives me the creeps," Virginia said. "Jenica never liked or trusted him. But he's always been fond of Eugene."

"If Luca knows something, he's doing a masterful job of pretending otherwise," said Virginia.

"Then you should try to keep reading him," Doina suggested. "We'll settle on some sort of story if he asks where Jenica's been. Maybe we should start following him. Jenica mentioned to me that almost everyone at the university was aware of him being a Securitate informer."

Mircea agreed. While many people in the university were listening to Radio Free Europe or taking part in the protests last year, others, like Luca, walked by the marchers and scribbled down their names. "There's no reason we should start telling people Jenica is missing or that we know something's wrong. It would put a target on our backs."

"We need to recheck Jenica's room for more clues. I'm going back to his dormitory tomorrow," Virginia told them.

"Definitely," said Mircea. "You need to take as many notebooks or memo pads as you can fit under your arm. Suppose we're ever going to figure out the cipher Jenica used in Bisu's note. In that case, we're going to need as much material as we can get our hands-on, starting with the notebooks you and Virginia have already found. If there are any phrases, numbers, or addresses that appear more than once, we'll compose a list of each one and try to figure out what they mean based on the context and what we already know."

"These could take hours, and I'm tired," Doina told them. " The wine makes me sleepy."

Virginia agreed. She put on her coat and almost headed out when she heard Doina shout: "Be careful! You know you are welcome to stay here with us if you want."

"I'll be fine. Thank you anyway. I guess I'll see you guys tomorrow after I search Jenica's room one more time."

Mircea shook his head. "That's the plan for now," he said and kissed her on the cheek. *She looks exhausted*, he thought, looking at Virginia's face.

Chapter Nine

Virginia had one more notebook under her arm when she walked through the door. Mircea and Doina were waiting in the living room. A big bottle of *tuica*, their favorite Romanian brandy made from plums, waited for them on the coffee table. They were all frightened and anxious, but looking through the notebooks and listing whatever patterns they could find had injected the group with a boost of optimism, as if the search itself, however futile, had made their work seem purposeful and worthwhile.

Mircea had increased his supply of Virginia's favorite variety of tea and readily poured a cup in front of her. This time, Virginia changed her mind and pointed her finger toward the big bottle on the coffee table. "I think I'll have a small shot of that if you don't mind."

"Oh no, not at all," Mircea said. "I'll have one also."

All this time, Doina was staring at Virginia. *Poor Virginia. After all, she's been through with her family, now this with Jenica? I guess some people can't get a break.* Doina thought back in time…

When she'd first arrived at the university, Virginia was still enjoying her victory in a domestic power struggle. Unlike her bookish and plain-speaking father, her mother, born Lucretia Borovici, had come from an old, artistically inclined family with roots in Bucovina. This region was a part of Moldavia. Lucretia was a poet who spoke fluent Russian and loved liturgical music and literature. From her, Virginia had inherited her perseverance and fighting spirit. After Virginia's graduation from a boarding school in Iasi, her mother had resisted her plans to become a doctor, which was at variance with Lucretia's ideas about the proper development of a wife and mother. Lucretia was a free spirit but quite conservative socially, and she didn't believe a hospital was an appropriate place for a young lady to spend her life. Alexandru's encouragement helped Virginia win the case. Many months passed before Lucretia relented in admiration of her daughter's persistence.

October 7, 1953, the date of Virginia's admission to the medical faculty, was marked by a sense of triumph, and yet Virginia's first year of studies was more devastating than she could have imagined. At the start of that winter, she received word that her father had fallen ill with tuberculosis. Even with the best medicine available at the time, the attending physicians gave little reason for hope. Over a few short weeks, Virginia watched as Alexandru's condition inexorably worsened until he died. Just a year after the passing of the most caring and generous man she had ever known, Virginia's oldest brother, Mitrita, came home after fighting on the Russian front. Life in close quarters with other soldiers and a lack of filtration for his unit's drinking water had exposed Mitrita to polio, and not long after he returned home, he lost the ability to walk.

It was around this time that Virginia and Doina became close. One of the city's more reputable doctors, Doina's father, visited the Gemanar home many times. Still, even for physicians with the best possible techniques at their disposal, the options for treatment were limited. Mitrita could not rise from bed; by Easter, he was dead. This second loss left Virginia in a state of excruciating despair, but she was also determined to put whatever energy reserve she still had into her studies. It would be a few more years before vaccines would become widely available. For a time, the young woman fixated on becoming a virologist or researcher in infectious disease, holding fast to the belief that she could harness the pain she'd endured into an engine of hope for other human beings.

In the summer months of 1956, students at the University of Bucharest, the Politechnica, and the Institute of Economic Sciences began hearing about protests in Poland and Hungary through broadcasts on Radio Free Europe. In October, a group demanding the "expulsion from Romania of Stalinists" took control of a local radio station. In November, after allied groups handed out antigovernment manifestos throughout the academic buildings, the Ministry of the Interior sent trucks and wagons full of armed soldiers to occupy University Square, preventing a planned demonstration from taking place. Although the events in Bucharest never reached the level of violence seen in Budapest, where the Soviet tanks overrun the cities streets, the Party response in Bucharest was severe. Students and faculty members who fought against the communist government were dismissed. The Securitate arrested thousands throughout Romania, and many people died in prison over the subsequent year.

These events had left a lasting scar on Virginia, who was volunteering at an oversubscribed hospital in the city's center. Day and night, among the smells of bandages and peroxide, the young woman witnessed an unending stream of women, men, and children with ulcers, burns, crusted sores, diabetes, malnutrition, heart disease, hepatitis, hemophilia, blunt-force trauma, puncture wounds, and food poisoning. For every ten patients who recovered, another ten took their place, and it was impossible not to think of the hundreds and thousands whom she would never be able to help.

Virginia's grief had a way of enhancing her thirst for knowledge even more—and she never gave up her taste for novels and poetry, even when overwhelmed by reading for courses in anatomy and pathology—but she treasured her education in medicine with particular ardor. Besides its empirical worth, the study of the human body has humanitarian, ethical, moral, and even create value. She held fast to it, above all, because she cared about making a better life for people.

Virginia slowly reacted to the student uprising by staying true to this one principle. Although these horrors never faded from her memory, and although there were moments when her capacity to trust and accept shelter from others seemed completely depleted, she began to let her guard down and started retaking risks with the urging of Doina. Perhaps she could never replace the sense of protection and innocence she had known growing up in her father's house, but at least she could try to leave the past in the past, make friends, and meet a nice young man.

* * *

Doina had come to recognize Virginia's method of running the ends of her scarf through the sleeves of her jacket before draping it behind the chair. They knew to wait for her to feel settled before she started talking, and they felt no need to ask where she had come from since her task was already settled: she was to look through each remaining notebook on Jenica's bookshelf and confirm that only the three they had collected contained the coded messages that needed decryption.

"This is the last one," she announced, laying the third notebook on the table. "I've looked through all the others, and now I'm sure. We'll have to see what contents it has in common with the others and maybe figure out the order in which each notebook was used, but I'm sure that there's nothing else of value in the notebooks I left behind. Everything is either lecture notes or paraphrased passages from Jenica's coursework."

Her two friends both nodded.

"Any other news?" Mircea asked her.

Virginia took her first shot of tuica.

"Well, there may be something else. I think I'm being followed. I keep seeing a guy with a dark tan coat around my apartment. At first, I thought it was my imagination since his features aren't that distinctive, and I could have confused him for someone else. I have tried to walk on different streets, and I have seen him behind me for the past few days—same hat, shoes, and dark tan coat, all impeccable. I almost confronted him on the street, near the university building, but once we were on the same block, I walked to the other corner and saw clearly as he stopped and started moving in the other direction."

"You did the right thing," Doina said.

Mircea seemed to agree. "It won't do too much good if you let on that you know you're being watched. Unfortunately, the only option is to be extra careful. Do you think he followed you today?"

"It's possible, though I practically walked backward for the last two blocks."

"Then we'll be extra careful too," Mircea said. He got up from the table, walked toward the kitchen, and peeked outside the window.

"Everything seems OK," said Mircea.

They all started going through Jenica's notebooks.

"Look at all these strange codes, flower symbols, and references to Carpati cigarettes," Doina told them.

"Yes, it's that strange flower drawn with three circles as the center and eight petals, just like in the message found on Bisu's note. Also, did you notice how many times these three letters—*FDC*—show up in the notebooks? They're everywhere near the flower drawing." Virginia had started to notice all kinds of weird things. She excused herself and went to use the restroom.

"OMG!" Virginia exclaimed. Doina and Mircea heard Virginia shout from the bathroom.

"Virginia, Virginia," Doina kept repeating while knocking on the door. "Are you OK?" When Virginia finally opened the door, Doina questioned her right away: "What in the world is wrong? You look like you just saw a ghost."

"Doina, look at my brooch...the flower—it's similar to the flower in Jenica's drawing. It's called *floare de colt*—FDC. Could this flower be the inspiration of the name of Jenica's organization?"

Doina was staring at Virginia's brooch. "You might be right."

They went back to the living room, where Mircea looked at Virginia's brooch. He had just finished writing down phrases, numbers, addresses, and, yes, the flower symbol.

"So what I concluded so far," he told them, "Jenica was having possible meetings with other people, and they were communicating using common code words and slogans."

"There was a name—Tony—a guy I have never met, but with whom Jenica apparently was working on a school project with a Professor Flueras. Mircea, did these names sound familiar to you?" Virginia asked curiously.

"I know Professor Flueras but never heard Jenica talking about a guy named Tony. But if Jenica was working on a school project with him and Professor Flueras, I might be able to find out something from the professor. I know him; I was one of his students a few years back. I'll check to see if he knows anything. What other patterns have we noticed in Jenica's notebooks?"

"The word *seed* seems to appear next to the phrase about the House of the Spark. We may not know how to translate it, but it's part of the code," said Virginia.

"Meanwhile," Doina cut in, "the line 'Three Gutenbergs' pops up again and again. It's written next to a set of two numbers. The first tends to be small and in parentheses. They seem random and are mostly between one and nine, but they're never bigger than triple digits. The second set is bigger and often a round number in the tens or hundreds. I saw lots of 50s, 120s, 200s, and so forth."

"Yeah, I noticed that too, Doina," said Mircea. "I think they might be purchase orders or maybe part of a formula for buying bulk supplies."

"Could they refer to pages in a book?" Virginia asked.

Doina and Mircea exchanged glances and invited her to go on.

"It's tricky to print a single volume on more than a thousand pages, especially if it's a text used by multiple students over a term since the binding is liable to break down. And I'm sure nothing on Jenica's bookshelf was longer than seven or eight hundred pages. There are versions of Iorga's *Opinions sincères* that are broken up into sections or taped together so they don't fall apart. Have you still got Jenica's copy?"

Mircea excitedly slid the book to the other end of the table so that it nearly collided with Doina's coffee cup. Virginia opened it and began looking up the page numbers from Jenica's notebook. At first, she found short, primarily three-lined quotations that were starred and underlined, many of which she had heard Jenica cite: "A people that does not know its history is like a child that does not know its parents…You can close your eyes, but you can't turn off the sun. The thought of death may serve you at any moment to understand the price of life."

"All these quotations are from Iorga's book," Mircea told them. "I know because I read the book a few times. Regarding the codes, I don't know what that means. We just have to use our imagination and see if we can come up with something."

As Virginia continued through the list of numbers, she saw the highlighted passages were longer and more elaborate and seemed to come together like bricks of a broad and impregnable wall. Gathering insights from the *Opinions sincères*, Jenica had built a rhetorical collage, using the most eloquent passages to make a clear and persuasive statement about the origins and cultural history of the Romanian people. Although some of the arguments were wordy or inelegant, reading the sequence was powerfully uplifting, like hearing a sermon or addressing a rally in Nation Square. The reflections that most often caught Jenica's eye weren't particularly antisocialist, let alone anti-Romanian, and evoked a vision for a peaceful, productive, and lawful country built on collective values and shared responsibility. Virginia found herself shaking her head at certain moments, unable to believe that such a book could be banned.

"It's like a pamphlet," she finally said.

Doina acknowledged in agreement. "Jenica didn't just want to pull these ideas together for himself. He wanted to assemble them on paper and share them with others in his circle. Those numbers in the notebook? Those *were* purchase orders but not for food or supplies; they are for a printer. The first figure is the page count, and the second figure is for the number of copies. That would go some way toward explaining the 'Three Gutenbergs.' I suppose they were printing subversive material in secret."

"But why three?" Virginia asked. "Maybe it's three printing shops? Or a shop at the crossroads of three streets? Or could the name of the printing shop have the number three in it?"

"That might be too obvious," Mircea said. "Though we shouldn't rule out the possibility that the printers were willing collaborators."

After tearing out a sheet of blank paper from his notebook, he sharpened his pencil and began to write. "OK," he said. "I guess this means another field trip. How many printing shops are within twenty blocks of the university?"

"Maybe we can find out at the library," Doina suggested.

"That's a great idea—the library that Jenica always used to study in," Virginia agreed.

* * *

Inside the library, Doina approached one of the librarians flirtatiously. "Sorry to bother you, but I would like to make a copy of some of my study material. Do you know any printing shops near the library or university?"

The librarian gave Doina the name of the three most used places. After she thanked him, she leaned toward his ear and whispered, "Nice pants."

The young librarian blushed and immediately returned to work. Doina smiled and walked toward Virginia and Mircea.

"What in the world did you tell that boy that made him rush away so fast, one of your dirty tricks again?" Mircea questioned her, noticing the boy's reaction.

"Not at all. Your jealousy is unfounded. I did find out the names of the printing shops near the library and university. Let's check them out."

"Let's spread out and meet at Mircea's apartment in about an hour," Virginia suggested.

* * *

Walking down Victory Avenue, Virginia looked longingly at the storefront windows. A beautiful-blue-dress display in one of the windows caught her attention. Seeing a man in the window's reflection, she let out a gasp. *It's him; he is following me. But how is this possible?*

She went into a cafeteria, bought herself a cake and a drink, and then sat at one of the tables pretending that she was just passing the time. Fifteen minutes later, the man was still at a nearby table pretending to be busy reading the *Free Romania* newspaper. Virginia got up from the table and walked toward him, seemingly accidentally dropping the pack of Carpati cigarettes when she pulled her handkerchief from her purse. The man jumped from his chair and picked it up. They looked at each other, and then Virginia rushed to exit the cafeteria.

"If you see the man again, don't give him the impression that you know he is following you," she recalled Mircea telling her.

She started walking again down the avenue, stopping to check the reflection in a window. She was not able to see the man.

"Thank God," she whispered and spent some time catching her breath as she looked around for the printing shop. "There!" The printing shop was not far from where she was. Her heart was still racing by the time she opened the store door.

"Hi, I would like to make copies of some study materials. Can you tell me how much it would cost me, please?" While she was talking, Virginia placed a package of Carpati cigarettes on the counter. She looked to see if the man had noticed. The man wrote down the prices and handed her the paper.

"Thank you; you've been very helpful. I will come back next week with my study materials." She was walking toward the exit when the store worker tried to get her attention.

"Miss? Excuse me, miss? I think you forgot your cigarettes on the counter."

"Oh, thank you so much. My boyfriend would be distraught if I lost his cigarettes."

The older man smiled.

* * *

In the meantime, Doina checked the printing shop near the La Rotunda bar.

It is way too close to the university, she thought to herself while entering the shop. Behind the counter, a young, good-looking guy noticed her.

"Good afternoon, miss. Is there anything that I might be able to help you with?"

After looking him up and down, Doina pulled a paper with some notes from her purse. She "accidentally" dropped a pack of Carpati cigarettes. The young man rushed to pick it up. Doina regarded his reaction.

"That's very kind of you."

She placed the package on the counter and continued to talk with the young employee. She looked at her watch. "Oh, look at the time; I have to go. Thank you for all the information." While rushing to exit the printing shop, Doina felt a tap on her shoulder.

"I think you forgot those on the counter." The young man handed her the package with Carpati cigarettes.

"Gosh, I am so forgetful. Thanks."

He leaned toward her, whispering in her ear, "Would you like to go see a movie sometime?"

"Thank you, but I am not available," she replied, showing him the ring with the bluestone topaz that Mircea had given her for her birthday.

* * *

Later that afternoon at Mircea's house, Doina was telling Virginia what had happened at the printing shop when their conversation was interrupted by Mircea.

"Why do you have to flirt with every man you encounter?"

"It was an innocent conversation. Are you in a bad mood? How was your visit to the printing shop?" Doina tried to keep it calm.

Mircea exited the room without saying anything.

Virginia stared at her. "Maybe I should go," she said, but Doina shook her head.

"Give me a minute. I'll go to find out what is going on."

"I wasn't able to find anything. The shop was closed, and I noticed some men nearby surveilling the store." Mircea rushed to tell her while looking outside through the window. He covered his face with both hands and raised his voice at Doina. "I need some time alone, please."

Doina raised her eyebrows. She looked at him then left her head down and told him;

"OK, then I will leave with Virginia. Call me tomorrow." She left the room without waiting for him to answer.

"What happened?" Virginia tried to open the conversation.

Doina shook her head. "Just Mircea. That's the way he is sometimes."

"But I thought that you guys get along well."

"Most of the time, it's just his attitude. His jealousy is killing our relationship." Doina told her, feeling annoyed.

"He is jealous because you get men's attention."

"Yes, you noticed that too."

"Mircea disliked your flirtatious attitude, Doina, but I think you already know.'

"Yes, I know, but to be honest, I don't care anymore. I told him repeatedly that even though I like the attention of other men, I haven't cheated on him."

"I think he feels insecure and afraid to lose you. You are such a beautiful and popular girl. He doesn't understand, Doina. He thinks like a man."

From the first day she met Doina, Virginia enjoyed her company. Doina was not only a beautiful girl with short black hair and big green eyes who knew how to dress to get men's attention, but she was also very kind and caring, always trying to help people. They nicknamed her Betty Boop at the university, and she likes it, but Mircea seems to have a problem with it.

"Doina, it's way too provocative. Can you just find some decent clothes?" Virginia heard Mircea's complaints a few times. Doina thought that Mircea became very controlling, and she didn't like that.

"I have no intention to change the way I am. He will have to get used to it."

Virginia tried to console her. They both refrained from talking for a while. Virginia reopened the discussion.

"Another dead end." She tried to hide her tears from Doina.

Doina rubbed her back. "We will keep searching. Let's stop at the store and grab some food."

"Good idea." They smiled at each other and headed towards the grocery store.

Chapter Ten

With a white towel around his waist and thin rubber clogs on his feet, Luca Moromete stood in front of one of the dorm's bathroom sinks, looking intently in the mirror. After running his comb under warm water, he re-formed the part in his hair and then fixed a rubber band around a fresh toothbrush, a thick tube of toothpaste, and a bar of deodorant. The hallway was characteristically noisy, and a steady stream of residents hurried in and out of the washroom, returning from a day of classes and preparing to visit friends or meet in groups at a cluster of nearby pubs. Luca, too, was looking forward to a drink with some boys he knew from his introductory geology survey—all of whom sat together in the back row during lectures, sharing notes or pestering the quieter students. After pulling on a long-sleeved shirt and charcoal trousers, he walked toward the stairwell.

The dorm lobby was very crowded. It took almost a full minute for Luca to find the people he recognized, and it would be another ten minutes before they could set out toward the pub as the last two or three friends made their way downstairs. Naturally, the friendliest way to pass the time was with sips of tuica. Luca had several, making him feel lively and even more eager to leave. He began walking toward the entrance when he saw a young woman his age on her way inside.

She had fair skin and blonde hair, long and held in a loose ponytail with a large tortoiseshell clasp. Luca noticed a baker's apron underneath her white-and-blue jacket. There was a nervous, out-of-place look in her eyes, and she was fiddling with something in her pocket. Walking further inside the lobby, she turned her neck in both directions as if looking for someone to meet. In another moment, she was stepping back to a lonely spot on a wall closest to the street, slipping in between two painted columns that ran from the ceiling to the windowsill.

Luca wouldn't remember much from the next four hours. He'd have three mugs of beer when he arrived at the first pub and three mugs more at the second, followed by a tumbler of brandy, a goblet of red wine he'd steal from a young lady who sat next to him at the bar, and two more bottles of beer. When he finally finished exchanging complaints about the geology professor, arguing about the outcome of a football match, and attempting to harmonize with strangers in a drinking song, he'd make one more trip to the toilet, light another cigarette, and begin wandering home. The lobby would be empty when Luca finally returned to the dormitory, and he still felt slightly restless and wondered what the girl with the baker's apron had been up to.

After nodding at the security guard, he used his last reserve of energy to examine the street-facing wall, running his eyes along the edges of each surface of the columns and through every crack in the paint. There was nothing wrong with the heavy metal bars that ran vertically over the windows or with the latch that held them closed. Nor was there anything unusual about the rusted panels that vented out warm air from the floor or with the smooth stone windowsill on which longer-legged students tended to rest their rear ends. He did, however, notice something resembling a matchbook in the heater grate beneath the window closest to the entrance, and when he looked closer, he realized it was a tightly folded piece of paper.

Retrieving a pen and a torn sheet from one of his notebooks in his pocket, Luca began to copy what he saw as carefully as he could. "Restaurant

Monte Carlo opens at 7:00 p.m., and they have plenty of Carpati cigarettes nearby." The message was a little odd but would almost certainly be the sort of thing that the secret police could decipher. What's more, beneath the text was a drawing of a flower with long, thin petals, which he was sure he had seen before. When he was done copying that as well, he followed the order of creases to fold the paper precisely as he had found it and put the note into the same wedge of the heater grate it had been in before.

When he showed his discovery to Professor Constantinescu the next day, they would figure out what the message meant. And whatever accomplices this traitor in the baker's apron was working with, when they convened at the Monte Carlo restaurant in Cismigiu Gardens, the Securitate would be patiently waiting.

* * *

Mircea went to the university and asked about Professor Flueras. Then he went to his classroom to have a conversation with him.

Professor Flueras seemed caught off guard when Mircea asked him about Jenica. "I'm sorry. What is your name again?"

"Mircea Greceanu, sir. I was a student of yours two years ago."

"You are looking for Jenica Cureteanu? No, I haven't seen him lately. I got word from others that something had happened in his family, and he had to go home. Do tell him if you see him that he needs to finish the project by the end of the month."

"I will surely mention it to him," Mircea told him before he left.

* * *

Back at his apartment, Mircea shared with Virginia his suspicions regarding Flueras.

"Virginia, you need to follow him. I have my suspicions. His hands started trembling when I mentioned Jenica's name. Maybe he had something to do with Jenica's disappearance. I am telling you he acted weird and rushed me out the door."

Virginia kept an eye out for Professor Flueras to see if he went anywhere. A couple of days later, she saw him going off campus during his lunch break. She followed him toward the Cismigiu Gardens. He stopped and sat on one of the benches near the Eminescu Spring. She waited and was about to leave when a man with a dog sat near him, and they seemed to be talking.

After the professor left, Virginia was ready to follow him when she felt a jolt of realization and exclaimed under her breath, "That's him, the man who has been following me! What is going on here? I am so confused."

She decided to keep it to herself and not mention anything to Mircea and Doina.

The following day, Virginia went back to the university and followed Professor Flueras on his lunch break. Trying to stay hidden, she noticed that he went eastward along the Boulevard Gheorghiu Dej and made his way toward the city center, crossing Coltea Park and stopping by the Church of the Three Hierarchs. Virginia was puzzled by his behavior. He simply wandered to a bench near the entrance where he sat doing nothing, lit a candle, and then went to the café next door. At the café, he quickly drank his coffee and left. When Virginia was sure he was gone, she approached the bench where he had sat in front of the church. She sat down and then rose and went to look at the place outside the church where the professor had stopped and lit a candle. She turned and look around. There was no one. She lit a few candles in her family's memory. She was about to leave when a drawing of a flower got her attention. Near the place designated for prayer requests was a small note with a flower on it. *She thought those prayers usually go inside the box, not near the box.* She opened it for a second and then hid it in her pocket.

Virginia hurried to Mircea's apartment.

"Yet another message," Mircea announced, holding the paper message open on the kitchen table with his pinkies and thumbs. "And we are in some agreement about what it means."

"We've gotten to know Jenica's system well enough," said Doina. "It looks to me like '7:00 p.m. at the Monte Carlo restaurant' in Cismigiu Gardens. And again, there's something about Carpati cigarettes: 'They have plenty of Carpati cigarettes nearby.' We haven't fully figured that out, except to say that it's a kind of greeting."

"Should we check out the restaurant then," asked Virginia, "like we did at the House of the Spark?"

"Sure. It's more or less the same kind of surveillance. The only difference is we'll have a chance to see a meeting before our eyes. Maybe. It'll be more dangerous, I suppose, but if we camouflage ourselves a bit, then we can finally figure out what's going on," said Doina.

Mircea shook his head. "You're going to hide in the bushes? Do you think we should dress in brown and olive-green fatigues, paint our faces, count to one hundred, and see if the secret police can find us? We've accessed a police detective bureau and trafficked in stolen evidence. Somebody is following us. Some of this might be attributable to the sheer incompetence of the people watching us. A lot of it is sheer luck. There's no reason to push it. I'll go by myself."

Doina looked over at Virginia, checking to see if they should pick their battles and consent to the supposed man in charge. Virginia held firm.

"If anyone is going to go it alone this time, you're looking at her. I'm the one Jenica was closest to. I have the most to lose if he's gone, and I should be the one who puts herself at the greatest risk. For all we know, that note was written and left at the Church of the Three Hierarchs specifically for me."

Now she was looking squarely at Mircea. "You said I should make the most of how little I know. If the Securitate took me in, they could question me for hours and use whatever methods they pleased—I would have nothing to tell them."

"We can't let you be completely on your own," he said and nodded at Doina. "She and I can hold back, but we'll have to be somewhere close by in the park."

"Sorry, why do I have to hold back?" asked Doina. "I should be with her."

Virginia shook her head, and Mircea threw up his hands and nearly stood up in his seat. "I'm not anybody's boss," he said. "I certainly can't tell Virginia what to do, but there's no reason for you both to put yourselves in danger. I'm begging you to stay put."

The notebooks on the kitchen table were spread out and shuffled together in a bigger mess than Mircea had ever produced on his own. His hair was oily, and he needed a shave. Virginia's second wind had ended, and though the look in her eyes was purposeful and explicit, her back was stiff, and she'd been wearing the same shirt for three days. Doina, the most robust member of the group, wondered how she could agree to stay home during the most dangerous undertaking of her friends' lives. But in another moment, she shrugged her shoulders and agreed.

* * *

At the other end of the university district, Mircea poured his bottle of tuica into three glasses: one for Virginia, one for Doina, and one for himself. After they'd made a quick toast, Mircea pulled his father's brown, cotton rain hat over his head. It was too small and tight to reach his ears.

"Wasn't it you who warned us about playing detective games?" Doina asked. "I understand you're trying to shade your face, but that hat is too noticeable." After another moment, she tried to speak in a more soothing tone, but it was too late.

"I'll wear my cap instead or maybe the hood of my jacket," Mircea said and looked over at Virginia. "What matters is you. When you head to Cismigiu Gardens, you can't give away that we're following you. You shouldn't try to look like you have any plan at all. I mean it. Be wary of anyone approaching you, especially if they ask you about Jenica. And if they do, you're to tell them you haven't seen him. Stick to the line about him leaving town unexpectedly to see his sick mother. Repeat it as many times as you need to, and listen closely to what they say in response. Meanwhile, all you're doing is enjoying a peaceful evening in a quiet park where you can find some clarity and think. If anyone asks you what you're thinking about, you must have an answer, but keep it vague. You cannot look like you're waiting for anyone. And you cannot say anything that might put yourself or us or Jenica in danger. I'll be close by."

Mircea tossed the too-tight cap onto the couch and pulled the lapels of his coat close to his chin. It didn't entirely cover his face, but it would have to suffice.

"I'll wait in the garden," Mircea said and then looked at Virginia. "I'll wait until you pass, then I'll follow you while staying out of sight. Good luck."

Virginia took several deep breaths. "Where are his cigarettes?" she asked.

Doina walked to a cupboard to the right of the stove, removed a pack and box of matches, and handed them both to Virginia, who lit one and took several hard drags, finishing it in less than a minute. Then she put on her coat and scarf and prepared to leave. Doina wiped a single tear from her eye.

"Will you please be careful? And it's OK if you want to back out."

"I know," Virginia said, opening the door. "But I'm going."

Doina nodded in understanding. "Look at what this country has turned us into. People aren't meant to live their lives this way."

Virginia turned back from the hallway. "Not this country, this government, this ideology. *We* are this country: you, me, Mircea–all of us. And we are fighting back, just like Jenica was fighting back. And maybe..." Her voice started to break. "Maybe we're never going to see him again. But he was fighting for this country, and so are we."

They hugged one more time, and Virginia walked down the stairs and out into the street.

Chapter Eleven

Light rain spattered the neighborhood around Cismigiu Gardens earlier in the afternoon. And the stone pathways were still glistening and wet. It was cold and dark when Virginia started walking through the empty streets near the park. She crossed the street and entered the gardens. The streetlamps were on, and although Virginia was expecting to be terrified, she found herself almost drowsily wandering past the first bench and the second, wondering if she was somehow getting closer to learning what had happened to Jenica. Half a dozen solitary men and women walked by her as she passed the pavilion. She thought of where Mircea might be hiding. Was someone waiting behind the hedges—a whole squad of Securitate perhaps, waiting to make an arrest? Was she about to meet Jenica's fate?

An older woman was selling cotton candy, Virginia's favorite treat growing up. She bought one and started walking near the edge of the park. She heard a rustling behind her and turned around. She couldn't see anything at first, though a shadow seemed to move. After a deep breath, she continued to walk until she'd reached the sidewalk and crossed the street. The restaurant was busy and full of noise, but no one was seated at the tables facing the street. Nor was anyone standing on the opposite corner of the intersection. All she could hear was the jingling collar of a leashed dog. Looking toward a row of naked linden trees, she remembered the perfume coming from those trees in summertime. Her mind drifted to memories of strolling along Victory Avenue or through Bucharest's charming old neighborhoods.

"You know, Virginia…a linden tree is one of the safest places to hide under during a thunderstorm. Its magnetism is so different from other trees," Jenica told her once.

The chirping of some late birds in the park brought Virginia back to reality. Mircea's instructions were still evident in her mind. Though they were interrupted momentarily by thoughts from her past—or images of Jenica's face as he sat in the library, deep in the study—she never lost track of the reality that she was in. She was waiting alone for someone she didn't know, whose motives were an utter mystery. She wondered how long she'd been waiting and looked at her watch. It was eight o'clock.

* * *

From the bushes, Mircea looked at his watch. He looked toward Virginia, who was still sitting on the bench at eight o'clock. It was then that he noticed a few figures moving. He looked down at Strada Romulus and saw a few other figures. More figures appeared on Popa Soare. They were dressed in uniforms and walked silently, keeping to the sides of the buildings and hiding in doorways. The Securitate was waiting. Mircea watched as the Securitate stood or paced in their places. They started looking at their watches, getting impatient.

Another group of men in uniform, this time the police (easily recognized by their blue uniforms), drilled the toes of their shoes into the pavement. A few of them walked around the park. They were smoking, and several were engaged in a friendly chat.

The Securitate stood silently in place, immune to distraction. Mircea saw them look at their watches and narrow their eyebrows with impatience. Around nine o'clock, the Securitate strode down the streets, trying other alleyways. Mircea watched them. They huddled together and began discussing something. The leader gave the group short commands, after which they broke off and started going door to door and into alleys, checking to see if any entries were open.

The park paths had grown so quiet that Virginia could hear men in café bars from five blocks away. It was getting cold. Her eyes were watery. No one had walked past her park bench for the past hour. She decided to wait for thirty more minutes, then go home.

It was nine thirty. Virginia sighed and rose from the bench. She hesitated for one more moment, then decided for sure that it was time to leave. No one had come.

Far away, from the window of a lake house tower, someone watched her through a pair of binoculars.

Virginia walked back through the park, toward the entry from which she came. As she approached the outside gate, she saw Mircea. She passed him and continued walking till he was out of the side park. She heard footsteps following her. She walked faster, almost running.

"Virginia, wait!" she heard Mircea yelling.

"They never came."

"No," Mircea said. "But I think someone was watching you."

Virginia's eyes lowered as she heard this piece of news. She flared her nostrils, took a deep breath, and allowed her jaw to fall into her chest, almost too exhausted to panic.

She wore the same look on her face the next day, sitting in Jenica's university café between classes and stirring the sugar in her cup with aimless, sputtering whirls. Above the door, a thin, metal bell chimed, and an older man walked inside, past a wrought-iron coatrack and a table arranged awkwardly next to the bar. The manager left stacks of day-old newspapers and a couple of decks of cards on one of the tables. The older man approached one of the tables next to hers. When he took off his coat, cap, and scarf, Virginia could see he had on suspenders instead of a belt and a matching

tweed vest, and he had thick, white sideburns beneath an almost completely bald head. He took a seat.

"Virginia?"

She looked up from her coffee in acknowledgment. The man was
short, had a round face and a shiny forehead. His eyes were very light blue,
and his cheeks were red. His expression was disconcertingly calm.

"You are Jenica's girlfriend, yes?"

It was at that moment that Virginia recognized the face of the man. It
was indeed none other than Professor Flueras.

Fearful that she might give something away, Virginia looked back
down at her coffee and did not reply. The older man reached into the
pocket of his jacket and pulled out something too small for her to see. He
held his hand out under the table and motioned for her to open hers, then
he released something made of metal that felt slightly cold. It was a silver
pin, sculpted into the shape of an edelweiss flower. Virginia was stunned.

"My name is Iulian Flueras. I'm a professor here on the history faculty.
I'm looking for Jenica, just like you. And I need your help."

Chapter Twelve

Later that afternoon, Virginia, Mircea, and Doina found themselves on a bus headed for the city's industrial section. After a twenty-minute ride, they walked down three side streets and into an alley. Virginia checked the address on a piece of paper in her pocket and then stepped toward the walnut-colored door and knocked three times.

"We're here to buy cigarettes," she announced to someone inside. "We've run out of Snagov."

They could hear a few moments of shuffling along a cement floor, followed by the lifting of the latch and the opening of the door. Virginia recognized the man who had been following her. The man stood in the doorway, wearing round-framed eyeglasses and carrying a small notebook and pen under his arm. He wore the same tweed vest with no jacket or cap and sat at a wide, oval, wooden table lit by candlelight. He motioned for them to come inside. After looking out onto the street in both directions, he closed the door, turned the dead bolt, and fit a brass hook into the latch. Through a short corridor and down a low-ceilinged staircase, the man then led his visitors into the warehouse's basement, where Professor Flueras was waiting.

"Welcome to the House of Spark," the man told them. Virginia, Doina, and Mircea raised an eyebrow while looking at each other but said nothing. Spread out all over the table was an array of stacked and rolled sheets of paper. A couple of them were as wide as a man's shoulders, though most were much smaller and could be folded into a small pocket without much effort. These were posters and flyers, with a few simple drawings of students marching and carrying signs next to large blocks of printed text. Virginia recognized a few quotations from Nicolae Iorga's *Opinions sincères*, a handful of which had even appeared in Jenica's notebooks. *So this is what he'd been working on*, she thought. How could they not have noticed?

"My name is Tony Dumitru, and I am the organization's leader called FDC," the man told them. Doina immediately recognized him from the description that Eugene made of him.

"I'll be darn," Mircea exclaimed while Doina rushed to ask him:

"What kind of organization is this? I assume anticomunist."

Tony shook his head in approval. "I was the one who recruited Jenica."

"Was Jenica involved in last year's protest?" Virginia cut through.

Tony looked her straight in her eyes. "Yes, Jenica started to get involved after I told him about the protest that started in Poland. I am sure you remembered the Poznan Protest from June last year. From the Free Europe radio station, we followed the events that later spread in Hungary. Students from Romania joined them. We all wanted the Soviet troops to leave our countries...." Tony stopped talking for a moment. "And we also protest against the totalitarian Communist regime."

"We are all aware of the outcome of the protests," Virginia told him.

"The name of the organization," Doina questioned him, "comes from the floare de colt? And what about the cigarettes?"

"Yes, the name that the Communist regime gave to the queen's flower."

Virginia touched her little brooch. It used to be Queen Marie's of Romania's favorite flower. The Communist people changed the name to floare de colt, trying to erase everything about the monarchy and downgrade its value. You see, we all came up with the idea of the drawing. The three circles in the center represent the three countries that rebelled last year: Poland, Hungary, and Romania. We were planning on a new protest.

But not a violent protest like the one that happened a year ago. We tried to create a nonviolent student movement that would force the government to pay attention. We were thinking of involving many students from universities around the country. That was where the eight-petals idea came from. They represent the eight cities in Romania where students were working in the protest: Cluj, Timisoara, Iasi, Brasov, Sighisoara, Targu Mures, Constanta, and finally Bucharest.

"Regarding the cigarettes, Carpati meant that the meeting will go on. Snagov meant the meeting is canceled," said Tony.

Virginia, Doina, and Mircea looked at each other and said nothing. All this was new for them. Of course, they could get some information from Jenica's notebooks, but what Tony was telling them was overwhelming.

"And there is more," Tony told them. "We printed all these posters and leaflets until our printer broke, and we had to stop. Then we got word that the Securitate had found out about our printing shop, and we had to move it fast. We named our printing shop The House of Spark. We weren't looking for glory as of the famous building, the House of the Spark that Russians designed. We were looking to gather people to find ideas to eliminate those invaders who took over our country. The name House of Spark symbolizes our country our ideas. That's why we slightly change the name from The House of the Spark. The House of Spark brings glory to Romania, not the Soviets. When we got word that the printing shop was under surveillance, we had no choice but to move it. We keep the spirit alive no matter how many times we have to move the House of Spark. You would be surprised to know that there were a lot of students interested in joining the organization and helping with the materials and distribution."

Tony took a break from talking to sip some mineral water (Borsec, one of Virginia's favorites).

Virginia was looking at the table full of leaflets. "How did you recruit students at the university with all the snakes working for the Securitate?"

"Recruiting was done by having casual conversation, with dropped questions to infer how the person was feeling about the economic rules that the communist regime tried to implement all over the country. Future 'tests' were applied: potential recruits had to succeed in passing a message to a specific recipient. The note would have a small drawing of the flower."

Mircea was looking at the table. "Wow, I knew nothing about all this."

"When was the protest planned?" asked Virginia, looking at Tony.

"The protest was planned for December 25, Christmas Day, when people were going to their friends and families or walking around the city trying to enjoy the holiday with each other—a forbidden holiday by the Communist regime. We were thinking that having the protest on Christmas Day would also be a symbolic protest against the regime, which tried to control people's beliefs, freedom of religion, and freedom of speech."

Virginia waited for Tony to stop talking and looked straight into his eyes. "You know where Jenica is? He's dead, or he's hiding, and you didn't trust his closest friends enough to tell us."

Professor Flueras was about to speak, but Tony answered instead.

"It's difficult to say," he said, strolling from the staircase and taking a seat at the table. "Our best guess is that officers from the Securitate had followed him, but we can't say for how long. Chances are, they've taken him in."

Virginia's face, which had been tinted reddish-orange by the candle-light, seemed to go pale suddenly.

"Is he still alive?" she asked.

Professor Flueras shrugged his shoulders. "I'm sorry," he said. "We really can't be sure. A month ago, there was a meeting between Tony, Jenica, Adrian Bisu, a young man named Alexandru Popescu, and other members who belong to the organization. We don't know exactly how, but the police and the Securitate found out what they were doing and staged a kind of ambush near the House of the Spark. Alexandru is small and inconspicuous and escaped with Tony. They both heard some shouting from out in the street less than a minute later, and they recognized Adrian's voice; after that, everything went silent. Jenica didn't show up at the meeting, so we don't know what happened to him. After hearing gunshots and the screeching of tires, Tony and Alexandru decided they were still in danger and needed to disperse. Jenica was the first to be compromised. Since his disappearance, we suspended FDC activity. We must stay low. We've sent Alexandru to stay with his aunt and uncle on the outskirts of town."

"He and I were fortunate," Tony said. "Given how much Jenica knows, there's a lot that interrogation could reveal. Meanwhile, we honestly can't say what happened to Adrian."

Virginia exchanged glances with Mircea and Doina. Mircea spoke up. "We might know a thing or two about that," he said. "The homicide report for a young man who fits Adrian's description was filed on the same day when Jenica went missing. Then the report disappeared. There's nothing in the records department at the detective bureau."

Professor Flueras looked at his belly. "Setting aside how you accessed the bureau records," he said, "are you sure the report is gone?"

"Jenica's uncle helped us initially," Virginia said. "He told us the body was Adrian's. We're no longer in contact, but he managed to retrieve a note Adrian had been carrying to the FDC meeting the night he got killed. As for the report, it has vanished. It's as if it never happened."

"Fine then," the professor said. "What I suppose that means is that someone in a very high position of authority was able to intervene. Whoever killed him has connections, and their reason for surveilling the FDC meeting must have been rather important. It's worth bearing in mind that not all political prisoners are treated with secrecy—nor, for that matter, are the people who simply get caught in the wrong place at the wrong time. Someone in the government is trying to crack down on protests and counterespionage that might undermine the regime. Make no mistake: FDC is up against a monster."

"We're sure you've met Luca Moromete," Tony said. "You have? Great. He's a Communist collaborator. We can never know these things beyond a shadow of a doubt, but the evidence is clear. One of our members left a decoy note that led the secret police to Strada Popa Soare and Strada Romulus corner, and they showed up in droves. I almost cornered myself. Besides that, we believe Professor Constantinescu may be a collaborator as well. But it's too soon to say how high up this goes in the chain of command."

Virginia peered over the table. "Is there anyone in Jenica's circle who isn't dead, behind bars, or impossible to trust?"

"I understand your frustration Virginia," said Tony. "We really don't know. The Securitate methods of repression infused most everybody with a feeling of fear."

"Eugene seems OK," Doina cut through. "If I had to guess, I'd say he's innocent. We still have to continue playing dumb around him, though; he may have pieces of information that seem unimportant to him but which turn out to be useful for us."

Mircea agreed.

"Tell me more about Jenica's uncle," Tony said. "Is there any way we can get more information from him?"

Virginia shook her head. "He and his wife are loyal Party members. Aurel is a colonel in the army and risked a lot by trying to help me. I think he knows that I am not telling him the truth, and he also noticed that the writing on the note found on Adrian's body at the morgue was similar to Jenica's writing. He clearly stated that he doesn't want to be involved in any way from now on. I don't blame him; his position and reputation can be affected. Nobody wants to get in the Securitate's binoculars."

"But there must be some way to get through to him," Tony was interested to find out.

Mircea, too, began to shake his head. "I don't suppose anyone is impenetrable, but we'll have to consider other means. So far, we have no clues on where the government is keeping Jenica. And you can't even be sure if he is still alive."

Professor Flueras pouted his lips. "If it's useful," he said, "I'll focus on Professor Constantinescu. He's made plenty of missteps so far, and there's a good chance he'll make another. It might be something about Jenica's whereabouts."

"I'll try talking to Aurel and Oara," Doina said. "Perhaps my approach will work slightly different from Virginia's, or they'll see my requests in a different light. I know Aurel has a crush on me. He jokingly told Mircea that I looked just like Oara when she was young."

Mircea stared at her for a few seconds. "It's worth a shot," he told them. "Meanwhile, I'll try talking to my cousin Dinu. Maybe he can find out more, but he's petrified too. He's been annoyed with me since I convinced him to break into the records room."

"What about Luca?" Doina asked.

Professor Flueras exchanged glances with Tony.

Chapter Thirteen

As the others soon learned, Tony was able to find quite a few bits of information about Luca from an old school colleague who was working for the Securitate but was against the regime. Jenica told Tony about a conversation between him and Luca one day. Luca told Jenica that he saw a poster advertising an FDC group that tried to spread new economics ideas around students. Jenica knew it was a lie. Tony never promoted the organization using posters. Tony was able to find out about Luca's past from the Securitate file.

He was born and raised in the Jiu Valley. Like most men in town, Luca's father, Vasile Moromete, was an avid drinker and worked long days in a nearby coal mine. His wife, Alexandra, worked in a factory to supplement his wages. More recently, she had taken work as a housekeeper in the closest midsized town and sold whatever extra vegetables they could spare from their garden to make ends meet. Until the 1930s, Luca's father had owned a sizable property in Walachia and made a comfortable living trading in livestock, produce, and dairy products. Although the family was never wealthy, they'd lived a dignified existence before the war and maintained strong connections to the land and its history.

After the Soviet occupation and Romania's entrance into the Warsaw Pact, all of that changed. The government took possession of the Walachia estate, and Vasile moved to the coal-mining district in search of work. In the Jiu Valley, it was there that his spirit broke, and he sought the comforts of cheap wine to numb the bitterness and anger in his heart. As Luca grew up, he witnessed his father drinking at all hours of the day, in varying states of weakness, spitefulness, and resignation. They fought often, and by the time he was a teenager, Luca was known to skip classes and hang out on the street with local youth gangs, smoking, and drinking among the neighborhood's pickpockets and petty thieves. Although his mother begged Luca to complete his education, Vasile agreed to let the boy begin working in the coal mines as a way of staying out of trouble.

Luca's time in the mines was immeasurably boring and rarely safe. For the first few years, he could envision no other way of life, but things changed sometime after his sixteenth birthday when a delegation of Party officials visited from Bucharest. The day before, forepersons and managing directors in the mine had handed out fresh uniforms for the workers to wear and allowed the men a few hours in the afternoon to rest and prepare. A small festival was held when the delegates finally arrived, looking well groomed and dressed in finely tailored suits. Children sang songs about the heroism of the common laborers and the glory of the People's Republic.

Luca saw a pen fall out of one official's coat pocket, and he scrambled to pick it up. The delegate, a man named Mr. Cioran, was dressed similarly to those of a small huddle of more important-looking officials, and he wore a gold signet ring and a brilliantly shining gold watch. He thanked Luca in a velvety baritone and struck up a conversation with the boy during a celebratory meal, where Luca's eyes moved persistently to the glint of the man's watch strap. Though the watch was a fake, no one in the Moromete family could have possibly known the difference, and to Luca's immense surprise, Mr. Cioran later offered it to him as a gift.

He asked the boy how long he'd worked in the coal mines and why he was not in school. He wondered aloud if the mines were a proper fit for such an intelligent young man and repeated many times that the Party needed an infusion of talented people with good ethics who could help guide the country to a stronger and more prosperous future. Saying he recognized Luca's potential, Mr. Cioran urged the boy to return to school and pursue a degree in philosophy, rhetoric, economics, or something similar. He said that membership in the Party could open all sorts of doors and handed Luca a business card with a Bucharest address. He added that he worked closely with the history and law faculty at the university.

Jenica told Tony about a confession that Luca made toward him a year ago. After meeting Cioran, Luca told Jenica he thought about how Mr. Cioran and the other officials were received and decided the world is divided into two types of people. First, some looked out for themselves, took the initiative, made tough decisions, and enjoyed the rewards. And second, there were those like his father—helpless dreamers who never escaped their frustration and despair. He knew for sure who he wanted to become and that no sacrifice would be too demanding.

Luca described to Jenica how his family reacted when he told them of his intention to give up his job in the mines and return to school. His mother and grandmother were overjoyed. His father, however, was openly suspicious, having seen the boy's interaction with Mr. Cioran. On a subsequent night, he consumed eight or nine glasses of tuica and beer and then began whipping Luca with his belt and demanding to know how a sixteen-year-old alcoholic could ever be allowed back into school.

"You want to be like those traitors and bureaucrats!" he screamed. "The people who stole our family's land? A derelict and a thief—and you somehow think you're too good for the mines?"

"At least I won't turn out to be like you," Luca snapped back at him. "Times are changing, and the future waits for no one. You're an old, irrelevant man stuck in the past. I pity you. And I refuse to make the same mistakes."

Professor Flueras recalled his first impression about Luca when he met him: "The boy was utterly metamorphosed when he enrolled in school. He arrived in the lecture halls early, sat in the front row, studied diligently, and asked plenty of questions."

Luca realized later that he could bully or cajole the brighter students into studying for him and completing his assignments. Soon he was trading stolen cash and shiny trinkets in return for these favors.

The boy who arrived in Bucharest to study law was solitary, ruthless, and allergic to shame. A high-ranking Party official, he thought, had seen something in him that no one else could appreciate, and he believed the time had come for him to rise above the disputes of his old neighborhood and embrace his position in the future. Luca's colleagues came to recognize his skills as a manipulator and profiteer. Plenty of his classmates were aware of how he'd managed to pass his university entrance exams with a minimum of preparation—but the esteem of his former friends carried little weight.

Once he was back in touch with Mr. Cioran, all that mattered were the Party sympathizers he could connect with within the university. Luca wasn't the best student; he was lazy and often passed his courses only through coercion, bribery, or threats to other students. Yet he took great pride in his abilities as a close reader and considered himself educated far beyond his years. As of late, all he seemed to care about were the things he could do, say, or promote to benefit the people who could help him gain a better footing. *Work, commitment, loyalty,* and *principles* were all just words.

"We must be careful around him," Tony said. "He's not only wily and intelligent but also selfish and cunning. He could be a silly mediocrity just trying to get ahead, or he could be something much worse. Right now, we can't be sure what makes him tick."

Chapter Fourteen

T he next day, Professor Flueras was in his office, pulling up his chair so that his chest fit snugly against the edge of his desk. Usually, he didn't mind looking at the term papers for his economic history classes, especially for the more advanced courses, where most of the students were bright and well prepared. But several submissions from this batch were frustrating to read; of about thirty young men and women, eight or nine had used the same turns of phrase, the same structure, and even the same full-length sentences in their papers on eighteenth-century industrial development.

When he suspected plagiarism, Professor Flueras took it rather personally, as if his competence and merit as a teacher were called into question. Weren't his lectures good enough? Hadn't he worked hard to lay out the material? Had he failed to make them understand the essentials? However, most of the papers showed a decent effort. Mixed in with the mediocre submissions and the flagrantly fishy work, Professor Flueras had found that a slim majority of his pupils could write adequately well and had reached a relatively high level of understanding of the material. Plus, there were also one or two who were quite good. Eugene Bratu, for example, had handed in a thoughtful, concise paper with an elegant structure, thorough citations, and no silly tangents or unnecessary flourishes. The article was exemplary, though it might have included a few lines of François Quesnay that Eugene hadn't fully digested. When he heard a knock at his door, Professor Flueras wondered if he had summoned the boy by telepathy. Eugene stood in his doorway.

"Good afternoon, sir. Sorry to bother you, but I was wondering if you can spare a few minutes and talk with me…or maybe some other time," he said, noticing the stack of papers that the professor had on his desk.

The professor stood up and waved him in.

"The hallways have been as quiet as the grave for the past few days," he told Eugene. "I suppose that's not so hard to understand, what with most courses in exam week at the moment. Was there something you needed to ask about your paper? I'm afraid you might have to wait for comments, but everything looks good so far."

"Not exactly, sir. I wanted to discuss something unrelated to your class."

Professor Flueras nodded and sat back down. He had some idea of what he was about to hear but didn't want to prompt anything or volunteer what he already knew.

"It can be confidential if you like," he said and then regretted the awkwardness. "Go right ahead."

Eugene took a seat and began speaking.

"A few weeks ago," he said, "I was at a p-pub called La Rotunda. It's just an f-f-f-few b-b-blocks away from the university, near the Cismigiu G-g-gardens…"

He was stammering. Perhaps it was strange to discuss drinking with a middle-aged instructor.

"I am familiar with the place. Some of my colleagues and I used to have lunch there. Their *mititei* are to die for. After the events last year at the university, we stopped doing this. The Securitate might get the wrong impression if they saw us socializing too much."

Eugene started to relax. "You know the place well," he said. "I guess I do too. In any event, I recently bumped into a fellow student there named Luca Moromete. His room is on the same floor in the men's dormitory as

I share with Jenica Cureteanu. He walked over to me as if to say hello, but instead of shaking hands, he said something rude and sarcastic and then walked away."

Professor Flueras pushed his chair away from the desk, allowing more breathing space.

"What did he say?"

"Something like 'Well, well. Look who's here, Jenica's new roommate.' My first instinct was to ignore it, but then I couldn't help but notice a scar and a bit of swelling over his left eye. When I asked him what had happened, he gave me a strange, menacing look, and we went back to our separate groups of friends. After an hour or two, I saw him again. He was sweating a bit now, and his face was slightly red. At the time, I was walking over to the men's room, but he sought out eye contact and then asked, 'Any news from Jenica?' It was in a tone of even more bitter sarcasm than before. Again, I thought it was bizarre but said nothing in response."

Eugene shifted in his chair and tugged at the short hairs of his sideburns. He seemed to have trouble sitting up straight. Professor Flueras stood straight up from his chair and got closer to Eugene. He tried to pretend he was calm, but he was a mess inside.

"I only started to get alarmed a few minutes later when I walked out of the men's room and was out of Luca's line of sight. He had his back to me, but I could see the face of the person he was talking to, who was pointing to the bruise above Luca's eye. As I passed his barstool, I heard him saying, 'Trust me, my friend. Whoever did this to me got what he deserved.'

"Then Luca laughed so loudly that folks could hear him from the other end of the crowded room. Half the people in the pub looked up from their drinks in confusion. I suppose people make all sorts of silly pronouncements when they've had a few beers, but I had trouble forgetting about what Luca had said. What's been particularly hard to explain, of course, is the coincidence."

Now, it was Professor Flueras who looked uncomfortable.

"Coincidence?"

"I haven't seen Jenica for more than two months now. Over the past few months, a couple of times, his friends or his girlfriend, Virginia, have stopped by to pick up books and drop them off. They've said he's taking an extended leave of absence from school to care for his sick stepmother, but it's just weird that Jenica hadn't contacted me at all since that Saturday when he was supposed to go to a concert with Virginia. I saw two tickets on his desk the night before. What makes me suspicious is the fact that at least once in the past two weeks, I've walked out of the washroom and could have sworn I saw Luca coming out of my room. When I looked at Jenica's desk and bookshelf, I was all but certain that something was out of place. Mind you, I'm just a first-year student. I don't know my way around, and I don't have many confidants in Bucharest or people who can tell me what I should do. I grew up in Constanta city. My father works for the post office, and my mother teaches art at one of the middle schools in town. Jenica is like a big brother to me. We get along pretty well. It's just not in his character to leave town without letting me know."

"You're a bright young man," Professor Flueras said. "I think you're right to be disturbed. What do you think has happened with Jenica?"

"I couldn't say. Everyone has heard of people picked up off the street for what they read or who their friends are, but it seems like a stretch to imagine Jenica as some kind of operative. On the other hand, there may be quite a bit I don't know about him."

"I suppose you should keep your eyes open then. Wait and see if Jenica comes back or if you notice any changes in Luca's behavior. We can't be sure how they're connected, can we?"

"I suppose not."

"Well, there you are. And I'm grateful that you should bring this to my attention, though it's not as if I have any special knowledge of detective work."

"Of course not," Eugene said, beginning to stand up. "Perhaps that's why I came to you. Last year, during the student protests, it was an immense surprise that so many faculty members were involved. Then there were others working directly for the Securitate, especially in departments like philosophy, rhetoric, or economics."

"Or history."

"Exactly. Are the faculty simply on call for the Party to help recruit young people while they're still completing their degrees? It's all too complicated for me to understand. All I'm sure of is that you're a middle-of-the-road kind of person, and I can trust you. Jenica always talked very highly about you, sir. Thanks so much for listening to me. And I hope my paper wasn't too much of a botched job."

Professor Flueras tried to smile.

"Not at all," he said. "Come by any time."

Professor Flueras took a deep breath and did not exhale until he heard Eugene's footsteps fade to the end of the hallway. He took a sip of cold tea and tried to return to grading the papers, but the sound of Eugene's words was still echoing in his head: *You're a middle-of-the-road kind of person, and I can trust you...*

By a strange stroke of luck, the professor had been on sabbatical during the student protests and probably knew no more than Eugene did about the subsequent faculty purge. Who could blame the faculty instructors for resenting a man who'd been on a quiet farm in Transylvania during the 1956 protests in Poland and Hungary and who was too busy practicing the violin and tending to his tomato plants to witness their reverberations in his home country?

Like the university in general, it had been a radically different place when Professor Flueras returned to Bucharest after the student revolt happened. He hadn't been there to witness the raid on the faculty offices or to see students and more than a few instructors being led away by the Securitate. Still, these events weren't impossible to picture when he caught a scornful look from a colleague who'd been allowed to stay. Walking the streets or up the stairs to the lecture halls on his own or washing his hands in the men's room around the corner from his office. He could figure out which of the instructors believed he'd collaborated with the authorities and which ones thought it was just a coincidence for him to have been resting in the countryside when their world had been turned upside down.

Professor Flueras had accepted the rudeness or distrust from a few colleagues. There was no way to prove beyond any doubt that he hadn't betrayed anyone in the department. In the end, the odor of distrust should not have prevented him from fulfilling his specific duties as an educator. By comparison, what had stung were the ways students too might have signaled their suspicion, either by sidestepping his lectures, forgoing visits to his office, or avoiding eye contact outside of class.

The professor was immeasurably grateful for the few young men and women who seemed to accept the professor's mentorship and didactic energy. When he first met Jenica Cureteanu—rather than listening and swallowing whole the truncated schoolroom chants about Romania and its history, formation, and culture—Jenica had introduced himself to their country's political economy through the writings of Cabet and Fourier, French philosophers who'd theorized ideal, self-sustaining communities of equal rights and shared responsibility. The boy could sound grandiose at times and take himself with the seriousness of sleeping giants, writing as if his words would leave a revolutionary impact on the way people lived for centuries to come. But wasn't that how students at that age were supposed to act? If you gave them vision and guidance, nurtured their talents, and corrected their missteps, there was no limit to how far they could go—so long as they accepted that guidance, of course, and recognized the missteps.

Professor Flueras knew how to recognize a pupil who had the skill and inborn discipline essential to being a good historian. He could also spot a charlatan from across a room. Long before he had heard Tony's report on Luca Moromete's family background, he had known the aggravation of having the boy from one of his degree-requirement classes for under-graduates. The boy's swaggering gait as he walked into the lecture hall had been a slight annoyance, and his uncomprehending questions had been a modest distraction. But what had gotten under Professor Flueras's skin was the obsequious tone Luca took during office hours. Between the obtuse comments about the reading, the boy seemed intent not only on charming his way into a higher grade but on somehow beguiling the professor into making a disparaging comment about the Socialist Republic that would attract the interest of the Securitate.

More than once, while crossing his legs and leaning back in a chair across from Professor Flueras's desk, Luca had tried to get a rise out of his instructor.

"Professor Flueras, what is your personal opinion on the manage-ment of heavy industry or the state-owned farms? What about currency inflation? Luca used to start the discussions with minimal grace and talk as though the professor was moments away from letting slip some critical remark about Stalin, the government, or communism as a general idea., But the professor had detected the traps with Luca and edged away from complex topics; then, he wondered if he couldn't see a tangible mark of disappointment on the boy's face. He had been unsure if that was just his imagination, but after hearing this new information about Luca today from Eugene, it no longer seemed possible. That little miscreant had not only embarked on a career in state intelligence but also decided to trap the most diligent, romantic people in the history department he could find. In other words, he wasn't only stupid and egotistical but also dan-gerous. After pushing a stack of papers away and pulling the telephone a little closer, Professor Flueras lifted the receiver and punched in a num-ber he knew by heart.

"Tony? It's Professor Flueras. I have some supplemental reading I'd like to show you. When's a good time for us to meet?"

Professor Flueras stopped at his house to grab a few of Jenica's manifestos on his way to meet Tony. The FDC chose Flueras's house to hide the manifestos. They thought that since the Securitate cleared him from the events a year ago and because he was the oldest FDC member and had a modest house, his place was the safest. But still, nobody was safe. It would be over for everyone if the Securitate decided to raid Flueras's house. They changed their minds to move them either to the warehouse near the House of the Spark or to secret hiding places around the city. The FDC decided there must be no hints about where they were and who was responsible for distributing them.

Professor Flueras and only one other FDC member knew who the printer was, and, even then, they rarely met in person. The weekend before Jenica's disappearance, they found a new printer. Unexpected news: Friday morning, the day of Jenica's disappearance, Professor Flueras received a call at 7:00 a.m. from the printing shop and was told, "Your second-year indexes are very popular, and someone took them by mistake." This was the code for "the shop is under surveillance." Professor Flueras was on pins and needles. As soon as he got off the phone with the printing shop, he called Tony.

Flueras was anxious. Iorga's essay was an essential printing job, and they did not have much time until the protest. However, he knew he had to trust the rest of FDC to do their job and trust their judgment.

When Jenica went missing on Friday, November 24, Professor Flueras ran earlier into Professor Constantinescu. He saw him walking out of the School of Law building and talking to Luca Moromete. Professor Flueras felt something was off about this but couldn't say why. Seeing Luca talking with Professor Constantinescu gave him a nagging feeling in the pit of his stomach that something was wrong, but he kept telling himself that he was overreacting. He was probably just spooked because the printing shop was under surveillance.

For the remainder of the day, Professor Flueras was somewhat distracted, to the point that some of the students noticed.

Going home from school that Friday around 5:00 or 6:00 p.m., Professor Flueras felt he had to tell Tony his feelings. When he got home, he hesitated. He didn't want to cause unnecessary drama and insecurity if there was no need.

He called Tony, made some conversation, and said, "When you come over tonight, please get me some cigarettes."

There was a long pause at the end of the line. Finally, Tony slowly said, "Which kind do you prefer?"

"I want the Snagov one. I'm just…feeling like I really could use a Snagov cigarette right now."

"Snagov," said Tony.

"Yes, Snagov."

Tony didn't say anything for a while. Finally, he told him, "It is too late. The stores are closed. Carpati is all I have for now."

Professor Flueras thought for a moment and nodded. "I think Carpati will be fine. Thank you."

He got off the phone with Tony and tried to empower himself, thinking everything was fine. He went to his desk and tried to focus on grading papers.

Later that Friday night, Flueras still felt uneasy but had essentially immersed himself in grading papers and calmed down a bit. Suddenly, he heard a strange sound coming from the window in his study room. The noise sounded like small pings, something like hail maybe, but hitting the windowpane directly. He glanced at the clock—ten in the evening.

He got up and went to the window. Outside, he saw Tony. Surprised, Professor Flueras asked him what he was doing. Tony indicated that he wanted to come in. Professor Flueras said he'd open the front door for him, but Tony shook his head.

The Professor started to panic. He understood that something was wrong and went and turned the light off and opened the window wide for Tony. When he finally was able to see Tony, he saw he was sweaty and dirty. His face betrayed desperation.

"What happened to you?" Right at that moment, Flueras felt struck by thunder. "The meeting…"

Tony rushed to tell him. "There was no meeting. You were right. We shouldn't have met. They got him: Adrian got captured. Jenica never showed up at the meeting. I am not sure what happened with Alexandru, Victor, and others from out of town. I was able to get away at the last moment."

Professor Flueras paled and listened in shock.

"Do you know what this means? They will be looking for anything that will arouse suspicion."

Professor Flueras asked him if he knew any friends or family of Adrian, Jenica, Alexandru, or Victor. Tony said he vaguely knew about Mircea and Doina, Jenica's closest friends, and a few others' friends. They realized that their friends would be looking for them. They decided to get a message to them without blowing their cover.

"We have to get a message to their family and friends without blowing our cover. And maybe we can find more information from them too," said Professor Flueras.

Chapter Fifteen

Tony stood at the intersection between the two arc-shaped paths in Cismigiu Park. He brought with him his black cairn terrier, Decebal, also known as his signaling device. The dog walked happily in front of him on his leash, unconcerned with the frigid weather as he left. He was always cheerful and energetic. He lapped up several gulps from a puddle that had formed around a broken water fountain near the meeting location. In the distance, Tony saw Professor Flueras approaching through a patch of lawn between two large elms. He was already seated when he came. The professor was wearing a long, heavy coat and a lamb fur hat on his head. A few strands of thinning gray hair blew in the wind. They looked around to make sure no one from the Securitate was nearby. Tony would have called the dog's name twice if they had been. Once they were confident no one was listening, Professor Flueras removed his gloves. They began to speak quietly, the professor telling Tony more information on the coded message he'd sent about additional details of Jenica's case.

"When we spoke last night, we discussed our suspicions of a young man who might have been Jenica's roommate last year. I wanted to tell you these suspicions are correct."

Tony was intrigued. "Who did you reach? Did you overhear something?"

"The source of information was Eugene, Jenica's current roommate. We were wrong; he's not as dense as we thought. He saw Luca rifling through Jenica's possessions. I think he was trying to improve his reputation with the Securitate. We're wise not to trust Luca."

"Where does this leave us?"

"It's likely Luca has further instructions from his connection at the faculty and will continue to trap people closest to him."

Putting his hands in his pockets, Tony nodded silently. "But how does that bring us any closer to finding Jenica?"

"It might not." The professor looked apologetic. "But my only suggestion is to avoid Luca and keep searching for the answers. I also brought you some of the manifesto Jenica was working on before he vanished. I hid them inside the newspaper."

"Tony reached for the newspaper and hid it inside his heavy coat. Thank you. I'll keep that in mind and continue searching for Jenica." Tony looked at his dog. "Let's go home, Decebal—got work to do. He patted his chest over his heart where he hid the manifesto."

Professor Flueras waited until Tony was out of sight before walking back to the university. On his way back, near the Eminescu fountain, he noticed Virginia on one of the benches, her eyes streaked with tears.

Trying to be upbeat, he said, "Virginia, what a pleasant surprise! How have you been?"

Virginia was still absorbing the events and futilely tried to hide her emotions. "Professor Flueras, I'm doing fine. I was just looking at the spring. Here, I met Jenica for the first time. 'It's time for you to drink from the "living water" of the great poet,' he told me."

"You know the story about the spring water?"

"Oh yes, we used to fill a few bottles with water and take them to Jenica's aunt Oara. She lives nearby. She was the one who told us about the myth going around, about the healing properties that people believe exist in the water. Jenica never believed it, but he loved his aunt too much to start a debate on the subject. I haven't been able to tell them the truth about Jenica being missing."

Virginia tried to hide her emotions, but it was too much to bear, and she started crying.

"We're all trying to find Jenica. I just want you to know you are not alone. Let's go have a cup of coffee—my treat."

"I appreciate that, but I need to go. Doina and Mircea are waiting. Thanks for the invitation."

"I guess I'll see you around. Keep your chin up, Virginia, and remember the sun will shine for us again one day. We can't lose hope, not after everything we've already accomplished."

Virginia left without saying another word. She paused in the alley to watch the professor drink from the "living water."

* * *

Looking outside into the dark from the bus window, Virginia recalled Professor Flueras's words: "The sun will shine for us again one day."

She was ready to ring the doorbell at Mircea's apartment when she heard a heated discussion. Doina was arguing with Mircea. Tired, Virginia changed her mind and went home. Later that evening, as she lay on her back in her bed, she was able to fall asleep without her nightly cup of chamomile tea or a glass of tuica. Her understanding of Jenica, his involvement with the FDC, and those following him made her feel a little less lost. It wasn't good news, but the calm of knowledge allowed her to peacefully drift off to sleep that evening.

* * *

A day and a half later, she received a different piece of information that didn't quite qualify as good news either, though it certainly wasn't the most unfortunate thing she'd ever heard. Luca Moromete was dead. Apparently, after spending several hours at a pub near the men's dormitory called the

Spotted Mule, the boy had taken a shortcut through an alleyway off Strada Ion Ghica and then walked between two parked cars on a one-way thoroughfare and stepped out into the street. There were no eyewitnesses, though a few passersby said they'd heard the crash from a couple of blocks away. A coroner's report had found a sizable cerebral contusion and significant damage to the middle meningeal artery—head injuries consistent with a sudden impact on the hood and windshield of a heavy, fast-moving truck. Whatever vehicle was involved, the driver had not stopped to see how badly Luca was hurt. It was hard to find tire marks on the pavement or any other indication that the driver had tried to use the brakes.

Mircea had arranged a meeting with Dinu at a café bar to ascertain the finer details of Luca's demise. The newspapers turned the tragic death of Luca into a satirical story about the consequences of excessive drinking. Still, rumors started around the university that Luca's death was not an accident but rather a Securitate punishment. He got eliminated because he started talking too much. Mircea tried to find out the truth regarding his accident, and that's why he once again reached out to Dinu.

"I have nothing else to tell you, Mircea. I do not doubt that the Securitate got rid of him. He started talking too much—not to mention his excessive drinking."

"I understand what you are saying. You know better than me how the Securitate operates."

Dinu sniffed and said nothing, got up from his chair, patted Mircea on the back, then whispered in his ear, "Sorry I wasn't able to help much. I'll see you around."

Mircea returned to the apartment. The smell coming from the kitchen made him forget for a moment the earlier news. Doina and Virginia were both anxious to find out what Dinu told to Mircea and were staring at him.

"I have no news," said Mircea. "Dinu just confirms my suspicion that the Securitate eliminated Luca. He knows better than me how these monsters operate. Luca was just too full of himself and thought that they protected him."

Virginia looked at Mircea and listened carefully to everything that he was saying. He was talking between his teeth. His face was pale, and his lips were getting purple."

"Let's eat," Virginia suggested.

After they began eating, Doina asked, "How is the stew, Mircea?"

"Very tasty, thank you. Was it you or Virginia who made it?"

"It was Virginia, of course. She used her mother's old recipe." Doina winked at Virginia and then signaled as though to make a toast, but she changed her mind when she saw Virginia's look. She put her glass down quietly. Mircea got up from the table, walked toward the window, opened it, and lit a cigarette.

Virginia tried to clean the table, but Doina stopped her. "I got this," she told her.

"OK," she replied, then got hold of her coat. "I am going home," Virginia told them. "I hope I can get some sleep tonight. I'll call you to-morrow," she told them before she headed it out.

* * *

Virginia arrived home and placed her keys on a plate beside the kitchen sink. Then the telephone rang.

"Hello…Hello? Who is this, please?" Virginia heard a dial tone. "What is going on?"

The phone rang again. This time around, Virginia was angry and was preparing to tell the caller to terminate the call when she heard words that would change the rest of her evening.

"I have a quick message for you." The voice sounded like that of a middle-aged woman.

"Whom am I speaking to, please?"

"It doesn't matter who I am. Someone locked in Jilava Penitentiary requires your support."

Virginia's heart sank. Almost everyone in Bucharest knew that the Jilava Penitentiary was one of the country's largest and most dreaded. The army had altered it into a detention facility and used it during the war. The army later converted it into a site for preventative and posttrial imprisonment for males who had been accused and found guilty of political crimes.

"How did you get this number?" Virginia asked.

"Today, while cleaning the interior of the building, I stumbled upon this number on the snow, on the prison courtyard, with the word *Help* after that."

"I am sorry, but I think you have the wrong number. I don't know anyone who is in prison there. Please, don't call me again."

Virginia's hands started to shake. The Securitate had stumbled on a thing and attempted to trap her. Of course, she could not trust the woman. What if this is all made up?

Then the phone rang a second time. The woman notified her that she risked a lot by just calling her.

"Ma'am, there have been numerous abuses reported lately. Furthermore, it is a lot easier to disappear from this place. If I were you, I would find out who might be locked there as soon as possible. Who knows? They might still be alive!"

"I already informed you that I don't know anyone who is locked up there."

While Virginia was preparing to hang up the phone, the woman on the other end of the line insisted, "Ma'am, listen to me. I know you not, and you know me not as well. I have no clue what kind of jam the person who drafted this note might have gotten into, but I feel duty-bound to relay this message to you. Bear in mind that many of the things I have heard of Jilava are accurate.

"Among others, the guards are cruel and negligent. Moreover, the directorship is unqualified. If I were to guess, quite a few prisoners incarcerated are no threat and should, in fact, be released. They should not even be in prison in the first place, save for the convergence of bad luck and accidents. Is there anyone you might think of that is incarcerated in Jilava?"

"No," Virginia replied. "Or I am not fully aware."

"I tell you, apart from that one word, the only other thing I could read was this telephone number."

"I advise you to promptly forget about who uttered those words in the first place."

"Good luck." The woman hung up.

Virginia was dumbfounded; her world began turning upside down, after which she collapsed on the couch.

She started repeating the words several times: "Jilava! Jilava!" With her forehead covered in large drops of sweat, she kept repeating, "Jilava! Jilava! How possible could that be?"

The terrifying place comprised black cells stationed underneath the ground, where those incarcerated suffer from the bitter cold and darkness, on nothing but a dirt floor.

Further to these, the incidence of food poisoning and unfiltered drinking water were rampant and frequently gave rise to infectious, with the lack of ventilation allowing diseases like tuberculosis to spread rapidly.

Virginia veiled her face with both hands and cried out loud.

"No, this is untrue." She knelt while crying and pulling her shirt to gasp for fresh air. She got hold of her coat and ran outside, repeating, "Jilava… Jilava…Jilava…I have to tell them." She was repeating again and again.

* * *

Mircea was awakened by a noise that emanated from downstairs. It was almost one in the morning. He grabbed his glasses and switched on the lights.

"Doina, did you hear that? It sounds like someone is hitting the door."

"Go back to sleep. It's so late. What's the matter with you? Why not just take a blue pill so that you can rest?" Doina replied with some irritation. A loud bang on the door made her jump off the bed—Doina's entire body trembled.

"Mircea, I think the Securitate is at the door. What should we do now?"

"Calm down. I'll go downstairs. You stay here. And say nothing if the Securitate questions you about Virginia or Jenica—we have not seen either one."

Mircea started shaking violently while his blood ran cold, but he nonetheless opened the door.

"Virginia, are you alone? What happened? Why are you here so late?"

"Mircea…" Virginia could barely say a word. "Mircea…I don't feel well. Jenica…" Then she collapsed in Mircea's arms.

"Virginia!" Doina came running down the stairs. "Let's lay her on the couch. Mircea, what is going on? Why is Virginia here?"

He gazed deeply, shock. "Virginia tried to tell me something about Jenica."

"Jenica!" Doina repeated. "How did she get here? There's no transportation at this time of night. Don't tell me that she walked here from her apartment."

"I can't believe it, but I think you're right. Look, she could scarcely breathe, and she collapsed in my arms before she could tell me what was going on."

They laid her on the couch and concealed her with a blanket. Mircea went into the kitchen to peek outside from the window's side, then lit a cigarette.

"I haven't noticed any activities outside," he told Doina.

"Mircea, why don't you go upstairs and get some rest? I'll stay with her until she wakes up," said Doina.

"All right! But if you need help, just let me know," he retorted to her while scaling the stairs toward the bedroom. However, after some time, he returned restlessly.

Doina had almost fallen asleep; Mircea's voice made her start. "I'm sorry, but I can't sleep. Let me sleep with you all here in the recliner. I promise that I won't say a word. I just want to be here when Virginia wakes up."

Doina swayed and nodded her head. "That's fine. I get it." She went into the kitchen and made herself a cup of warm tea.

Virginia slept the whole night. It was almost eleven in the morning when she eventually opened her eyes. The intense light coming from outside made her repeatedly blink her eyes. "What time is it? Doina! Why am I here at your house?" she asked, barely able to speak. Her face was ashen, and she looked confused.

"You don't remember? You came here last night. Mircea told me that you said something about Jenica before you fainted in his arms. How could you walk here in the middle of the night by yourself? Do you know how dangerous that can be?" Doina snapped at her.

Virginia veiled her face with both hands sobbing, shouted out loud, "I think I know where Jenica is!"

Doina and Mircea exchanged looks but said nothing. Virginia found the strength to keep talking, "I think Jenica's locked at Jilava."

"Jilava! Jilava? How can you be so sure?" Mircea rushed to ask her.

"I'm not, but a woman who called me last night is sure that someone locked in Jilava needs my help—that someone I know is locked at Jilava. The person had no option but to risk my life by writing my number in the snow inside the prison courtyard."

"Virginia, this is outrageous. What if it's a trap? Could the Securitate have discovered that we searched for Jenica and crafted this fake narrative?"

"To tell you the truth, I thought the same thing. But the woman was so convinced that someone took the risk to reach me. I really think that Jenica could be the one imprisoned there. However, I just don't know how possible it is to end up in Jilava. She insisted that I needed to do something as soon as possible because of all kinds of atrocities; it's hard for someone to survive in that place for long. Mircea, if Jenica is locked in that prison, we can't wait too long," she insisted. "There is only one person I could think of that might be able to help me." Virginia got off the couch and started to walk toward the door.

"Yeah, right! Do you think that Jenica's uncle is going to assist you? Good luck with that!" Mircea shook his head.

"I'm left with no other option. Do you have a different idea? I'm personally open to anything. If Aurel made some inquiries, he could ascertain whether Jenica is indeed at Jilava. We have to lay out the complete truth to Oara and Aurel."

"Virginia, I'll go with you," Doina began to put on her shoes and dashed to comb her hair.

"I have to change my clothes. Is it all right if I borrow some of yours, Doina?"

"That would not be a problem, but I have a better idea. Why don't we go to our apartment? Then we can take a bus straight to Jenica's aunt and uncle's apartment. We actually live closer to them than Mircea."

"Yeah, let's do that." They were preparing to go when Mircea stopped them at the door.

"Whoa, whoa, not so fast. What about me? You know that I'm a favorite of Oara. I'm like an adopted son."

Virginia and Doina looked at each other.

"I need an answer, please."

"Fine, if that's what you prefer. But you have to buy them two savarine." Doina mustered a smile. She knew the Romanian syrup cakes with a whipped cream filling would soften the aunt and uncle toward them.

"OK, I can do that; I just need a little bit of time to buy the savarine. Let's meet at five o'clock in front of their building. I know the address, Virginia. I've been there quite a few times with Jenica."

"That's completely fine with us. Please try not to be late, and thanks in advance." Virginia tried to sound upbeat, but she was still spinning inside.

"Sure, I shall try my best." Mircea walked away while mumbling, "Women…can't live with them; can't live without them."

Virginia put on different clothes as Doina packed a small bag to carry along with her to Mircea's apartment.

"You forgot your edelweiss pin," Doina noticed.

She turned around, went into her room, and grabbed it. "I hope this is not a bad omen."

"Let's not give up so easily. I'm sure Aurel will want to help—if not for Jenica, maybe for Oara."

"I hope you're right. Aurel doesn't like Jenica's anti-communist ideas. Oara forbade them both to talk about politics while Jenica was visiting," said Virginia.

"Let's just hope that Aurel will have a change of heart and will help us to find Jenica," said Doina closing their apartment door.

Chapter Sixteen

Five in the afternoon was rush hour. It, therefore, took them rough-ly one hour to get to Oara and Aurel's house. To their amazement, Mircea was waiting, holding a white package in his hands.

"Ladies." He welcomed them and took hold of Doina's bag.

They all gazed at each other and nodded.

"Let's try. What do we have to lose?" Virginia opened the outer door for the two of them.

"Let's keep our fingers crossed." Doina gazed at Mircea. She tried to smile and rang the bell.

Oara opened the door.

"Oh my! Look who is here—Mircea, Virginia, and Doina." Oara at-tempted to peek into the hallway to ascertain whether Jenica was there. To her absolute amazement, he was absent. She rushed to ask Mircea, "Jenica…Where's Jenica?" she stammered. "I was looking forward to see-ing him."

Even though Mircea knew the savarine cakes wouldn't help soften the news they were about to deliver, he held up the package. "I brought your favorite cake."

Aurel's face popped into the doorway; he was clearly surprised to see them all. "Get inside, all of you, and tell me what brings you here unan-nounced." He ushered them into the living room.

Aurel gazed straight at Virginia and nodded his head in encouragement. She began to talk.

"Sir, do you recall the piece of paper you gave me from Adrian's body? You were correct; the writing on the paper was indeed Jenica's. I did not want to tell you the truth because I didn't want you and Oara to worry, and I was hoping to find Jenica on my own. I was wrong. Jenica has been missing for well over two months now."

Aurel stared at her. He was not happy at all. He knew it was Jenica who had drafted the paper, but his mind had not been able to accept the fact.

"Virginia, what do you mean he is missing?" Oara asked.

"Nobody has seen him for more than two months. We had planned to meet in front of the Mihai Eminescu statue on November 25. You probably know the statue located in front of the Athenaeum. We were supposed to go to a concert, but he never came. We have been searching for him ever since."

"He has been missing for two months? How is it possible?" Oara asked. "Mircea, do you think it has to do with the protest from last year?"

"Honestly, I don't know."

"Last night," Virginia continued, "I received a call from a strange woman who claimed to be working at Jilava prison. She saw my number written in the snow inside the prison courtyard, followed by the word *help*. I think Jenica is locked at Jilava, but I could be wrong since I don't have any other information." She turned and faced Aurel. "We need your help to find out whether Jenica is locked up there or not. You are our only hope in this. Sir, please help us find your nephew, Jenica."

"Jenica." Aurel shook his head. "I told Oara a long time ago that he is always courting trouble. His possibly ending up in Jilava has never crossed my mind, though." He paused. "This is very dangerous what you have asked me to do. I don't promise anything," he said, staring at the floor. "You all need to leave now."

They were at the door when Aurel shouted out loud, "Virginia!"

"Yes, sir?"

"I will call you," said Aurel. "Jenica…Jenica…" he mumbled, shaking his head.

Oara walked up to him, wiping her tear-streaked face on her apron.

When he rose from the recliner, Aurel's face was red, mumbling, "These young people—" Oara cut him off.

"---Aurel, you have to do something. I know you and Jenica barely agree on anything, but he is my deceased sister's son. I promised Cornelia a long time ago that I would look after him if something happened to her. I lost her, but I can't lose Jenica also." Her speech was wavered and broken.

Aurel started walking around the room with his hands behind his back. He was really disturbed by the unexpected news, but he tried to hide the gravity of the situation from Oara. *I can be in really big trouble if the Securitate finds out that we are related*, Aurel thought. He knew that if Jenica was indeed the one locked at Jilava, his survival chances were minimal.

Aurel walked toward her. "If I find out he's in Jilava, you need to take the first train and go to his parents. They need to know right away what happened; they could also be in danger. You never know what these people might do. He knew better than to mess with these people.

"The Securitate!" he shouted out loud. "This boy is insane! I tried to warn him a few times, but he listened to me carelessly. We can't get involved or let them know we're related. I could lose my job, or we could both get arrested. I'm sure he did something foolish because they're only the worst criminals who are locked up in that dreadful place." Seeing the sad look on her face, he tried to soothe her. "I'll see what I can find out tomorrow. But don't mention that our nephew is missing or worst that he might be locked at Jilava to any members of the party."

"I won't; just promise me you will try to find out what's going on."

"I promise, but that's all I can do for him. I am sure you understand that it is too dangerous to get involved and try to save him." He reached out to hug her.

"I'll be fine," she said through tears. "Thank you for doing this."

She kissed him on his cheek, then went into the kitchen.

"I will go and tell Ionita if we find out that he is there. Oh, what a nightmare." She looked outside the window at the city. She let out a sound of pain.

Aurel tried to comfort her. "I'm going to try to come up with a plan. Try to get some rest," Aurel told her, attempting to keep a calm demeanor. Inside, he was fuming. He stopped and looked at Jenica's picture hanging on the wall in the hallway. "What did you do, Jenica?"

Despite Aurel's feelings, Oara loved Jenica unconditionally. She talked about him often with friends, describing him as a young man full of ambition. "Jenica has many of his mother's best qualities: a fighting spirit, courage, and the ability to rise over setbacks," she used to describe him to others.

While attending Alexandru Vlahuta Boarding High School in Arad, he had learned his mother was sick. His father, Ionita, had shown up at the school one day, saying, "Get your stuff; we need to go." They got on a train and went to Bucharest, where they went directly to a hospital. Once there, Jenica looked at the woman lying on the bed.

"Mom, Mom, what happened?" By the time Jenica arrived at the hospital, she couldn't understand what was happening around her or recognize people. She died a few minutes later. The doctors told them that Cornelia had died from stomach cancer.

Even though watching his mother die was one of the most devastating moments in his life, Jenica pushed through and graduated high school. After graduation, Jenica wanted to go to college, but his father was against the idea. He wanted Jenica to become a farmer just like him. They began to argue every day.

Although Jenica loved his father, everything about the two men was different.

"Jenica, listen to me. You have everything you need right here. Boy, look around you. This farm is yours. Why on earth do you want to go to college? Do you want to spend all your life locked inside a place, just like your grandfather?"

"Dad, I am not a peasant! When are you going to understand? These days, parents encourage children to go to school to have a better life, and this was Mother's wish. She always encouraged me to go to college."

"You are just like your grandfather," Ionita always used to say to finish their argument. "Just like your grandfather."

Ionita was born in Transylvania to Austro-Hungarian parents Nicolae Cureteanu and Ana Moran. His father worked for the Romanian press as the editor of a bilingual magazine, *Unirea*. His mother was a teacher. Ionita was the youngest child and only son, a rebel at heart and the opposite of his sisters. He rejected lessons at school, especially learning languages, refusing to learn Hungarian instead of Romanian. When his father tried to explain the importance and the history of Transylvania and the Austro-Hungarian people, Ionita responded by saying it was a grave insult. Nothing they said made Ionita care. Each day was a struggle for Nicolae and Ana to persuade him to attend school. Passionate by nature, the boy seemed to enjoy nothing more than walking along the river, fishing or swimming in the freezing water, or lying in the grass in a spacious meadow, daydreaming while looking at the sky. Despite his mother's concern, Nicolae believed nothing was alarming about his son's behavior. Ionita adored his father, even though Ionita was the black sheep in the family. But he never understood how his father could be happy and satisfied spending so much time reading and writing.

One day, Nicolae promised Ionita they would go fishing. Sadly, he broke the promise, once again prompting his son to ask how the older man could never be bored with articles and books. He laughed at first and then began to explain the benefit of increasing one's general knowledge or acquiring a better understanding of cultures worldwide, even adding a few details about the impact of Hungarian poetry and art on the history of Europe at large. Still, Ionita was unconvinced, and he never forgot the offense.

After his father's unexpected death, Ionita took control of his future. He ran away from home to live with his uncle Miron in Draut. When he arrived, his uncle was shocked to see him at his door. He was even more upset when he learned Ionita had run away from home, knowing that Ana would blame him for her son's behavior. Despite Ionita begging him not to, he reached out to her. Ana didn't blame him. She was tired of Ionita's attitude and asked if Miron would let him stay. Miron was happy to help her out. He understood that caring for five children by herself was not an easy job. He saw much of himself in his nephew; however, he resisted telling Ana that.

"This is only temporary, Miron, and make sure that Ionita goes back to school."

"Yes, ma'am."

Ionita did go back to school, but his behavior never changed, and he struggled to finish tenth grade. One day, he dropped out of school.

"Uncle Miron, I've decided to go find a job," he told him.

"Ionita, you don't have any qualifications, and you are only fourteen years old. Where are you going to find a job?"

"I'll find a job. You watch."

He started working and often changed jobs. Miron got very worried when he became involved with rebel teens in the village. The third time, police brought him home. They told his uncle, "Miron, this is the last time that we will bring him back to you; he was drinking and started a fight with Gheorghe's son near the bridge. Next time, we'll take him to jail. Make sure he understands that."

"Don't worry. I'll teach Ionita a lesson to remember for the rest of his life." Miron took his belt and hit him.

"You are not going to end up in jail. From now on, you will come to work with me every day," he told him.

Ionita tried to fight him, but Miron was much stronger than him and stopped him. Ionita refused to do anything for the next few weeks, just laid in bed. Miron got mad and told him to pack his stuff and return to his mother. He wasn't talking seriously, but he wanted to teach Ionita a lesson. It was then that rebel Ionita realized right away that his uncle, who'd never hit him once in all the years they had lived together, was serious. Hence, Ionita settled to work in the forestry business, helping his uncle.

The Romanian economy after World War I had been set back all over the country. The Hungarian-Romanian War started in November 1918 and ended in August 1919 with a Romanian victory. Transylvania returned to Romania. A year later, under the Treaty of Trianon, the city of Arad was ceded to Romania. Ionita couldn't be happier. Overwhelmed, he looked up to the sky. "It happened, Dad. I wish you were here." He recalled a long conversation with his father, who anticipated this outcome for Arad and the entire region of Transylvania many years ago.

After the war, Romania, the country that used to be called "the bread-basket of Europe" for being a significant grain exporter, had to import grain to meet the population's urgent needs. Even though Romania had won the war, the results were devastating, and many people died or became invalids. Peasants lost their farm animals (cattle, horses, pigs, and sheep). When Miron returned from the front, he saw his farm devastated. Ionita was able to survive by hiding in the forest along with other peasants from the village.

A short time after the war, Miron learned of a new reform taking place all over the country called "the change of land ownership." Miron took advantage of this redistribution of ownership and chose some land for Ionita near the village entrance. The day he signed the paper for the land, Miron wrote a long letter to Ionita's mother explaining that school was not for everyone, but this didn't mean that the person who refused to go to school was terrible. He just thought differently. Ionita, in Miron's opinion, was just like his father—deep in thought and firm in his beliefs and decisions. But Ionita was different: he wasn't simply looking at the world; he was observing it closely.

Ionita grew up to be a farmer who was admired by many. His house was one of the most beautiful and modern in the village. Many people were jealous, and after the Communist regime took over the country, they tried to take everything from him. Ionita was knowledgeable, despite never having gone to college, and knew how to play the system by bribing authority figures in the village to protect his family and farm. Later in life, Jenica recalled his father's advice: "Jenica, sometimes you need to walk with the devil until you've crossed the bridge." One thing was indeed true: Ionita won the battle against the Communist regime.

Jenica's stepmother was the one who convinced Ionita to let Jenica go to college. And Oara helped by telling Ionita she would look after him. Since she and her husband, Aurel, lived in Bucharest, they offered Jenica a place to live. Jenica politely refused their offer since Aurel was heavily involved with the Communist Party, which Jenica opposed.

It wasn't easy to transfer from the University of Cluj to Bucharest, but Jenica was determined. Finally, he received his acceptance letter. All his hard work had paid off, and he was off to college in Bucharest, a city he thought was the most idyllic in Romania. Once there, he found Cismigiu Gardens, where he spent most of his time between classes. He spent many days sitting on one of the benches in Eminescu Spring, reading a book or daydreaming.

When he moved to Bucharest for college, Jenica, like his father, became critical of the Communist revolution. He embraced the ideas of Iorga, who described Stalin as a dangerous "usurper." He joined the FDC organization. He expressed alarm about the Romanian Communist Party for its terrorism and foreign nature. Moreover, he loathed the brutal methods the Securitate had used the previous year to stop the students' movement.

Chapter Seventeen

Two weeks had passed since Virginia went to Aurel and Oara's house, and there was no news from them. Then one day, the phone rang. She rushed to answer.

"Hello? Who is this? I'm happy you called, sir. Do you have news about Jenica?"

She heard a pause in his voice as if something might be wrong. "Are you home alone?" As he asked, the doorbell rang. Virginia asked him to hold on so she could answer. It was Mircea and Doina.

"Aurel is on the phone," Virginia let them know. "Thank you for waiting; I have Mircea and Doina here with me. Please tell me. What did you find out?"

"That's good." Aurel paused. "I've learned Jenica is locked in Jilava."

Virginia started to swoon and dropped the phone. Mircea caught it before it hit the ground. "Sir, hello, sir it's Mircea. I overheard you saying that indeed Jenica is locked at Jilava."

"Yes." A loud noise interrupted their conversation. "Mircea, I have to go. We'll talk soon." He hung up the phone before Mircea could say goodbye.

Virginia got up and walked into the other room, crying. Doina looked at Mircea. "This is crazy. How could this have happened?" Mircea shook his head but said nothing.

Mircea learned from other colleagues the terrible condition and abuse that was happening at Jilava. The imprisoned men were hardly allowed to get out of their cells, save for sessions of their hard labor in the yards—to lift stones and move them from one place to another or to dig trenches in the soil and refill them, all while the communications were severely restricted.

Meals were delivered to the cells once per day in utter silence. The thick walls of the cells impeded the inmates from shouting their messages to each other or sending out written correspondence to the outside world.

A long hour passed. Doina and Mircea could hear Virginia crying in the other room as they sat in silence. "Let's give her some space, and then we can come up with a plan for what to do," said Doina.

A few hours later, the doorbell rang; it was Aurel. He didn't say a word. He just went to the window, opened it, and lit a cigarette. After a few long draws, he let them know why he'd come. "I found out some more information. He's already been tried, convicted, and sentenced to life in prison."

Mircea shook his head, disbelieving what he'd just heard. "I don't believe it. That can't be possible so quickly." All of his questions came out in a jumble. "What are his charges? Could you be mistaken?"

Aurel's face didn't hide his irritation. "No. I'm not," he said shortly. "I know this isn't what you wanted to hear, but it's the truth. Oara has already left to see his parents this afternoon." He paused to light another cigarette. "I dropped her at the train station. This situation is not only complicated but also risky. I told her I didn't think I could help him since he was convicted, and I don't think a lawyer will take his case."

Mircea was not ready to give up. "We have to do something. It's not like we can let him…"—he paused, choking on his words—"*die* there. Did you find out about his charges?"

"No, the Securitate seized his file. I can guess that since it's Jilava, his charges are political."

Virginia stood in the doorway to her room, tears still cascading down her cheeks. Aurel spoke to her, much softer than he had to Mircea. "I am so sorry. I know this is a terrible situation and hard to take in. I wish there were more we could do for him, but I said as much to Oara." He touched her shoulder lightly as he walked by. "I didn't sleep very well last night. I need to go. Oara loves him so much. She cried all night. It's breaking her heart to know he's behind bars." He walked out the door without another word.

Doina spoke after he left. "I don't even know what to say anymore. We just have to wait and see what Jenica's parents decide."

"Yeah," Mircea agreed. "I'll try to find out more pieces of information."

* * *

Draut, the village where Jenica's parents lived, was situated near the Hungarian border. Since her sister's funeral almost five years ago, Oara never returned to their village. It took her more than eight hours to reach the city of Arad, from where she was supposed to get the bus to the village. Once she reached Arad, she noticed how much the town had changed; tall buildings had sprouted up all over. She spent the train ride thinking about what she would say when she got there.

I will stop at the church to rest, she thought. She and Jenica's mother, Cornelia, attended the Sunday services years ago.

"Where is the church?" Oara was confused. She stopped an older woman, dressed in traditional clothes from Ardeal, to ask for directions.

The older woman looked at her, surprised. "I can tell you are not from here." Then she walked away without answering her question.

Oara got upset. She stopped an older man. "Excuse me, can you tell me which way is Santa Ana church?"

"The devils destroyed the church, dearie!"

She looked at him, confused. "What devils?"

"The Communist people," he told her, staring at her.

Oara couldn't hide her shock. She recalled the conversations between the members at the Party meetings; they profoundly believed that communism and religion couldn't coexist. Their intentions were indeed to destroy all the country's churches. She had quickly dismissed the thought because she didn't believe it could happen. Apparently, the plan to demolish the churches was delayed in Bucharest because not everybody agreed with the idea. That was not the case in other parts of the country. "Religion is the opium of the people and needs to be erased," Oara recalled one of the members quoting Karl Marx to convince those who would listen. The harsh reality unveiled in front of her; a park took the place of her beloved church.

Despite being tired and full of disappointment, she continued walking down the road. She thought she had seen enough for one day and would catch the bus to go to the village. Luckily, she spotted a bus coming toward her. She waved at the driver, trying to get his attention.

"May I help you?" A young man approached her.

"Good evening, sir. I am trying to get to Draut village. Is this the right bus?"

"Yes, ma'am."

She rushed onto the bus.

"Ma'am, the bus is full, but Draut is the first stop. Just stay by the door," the driver told her.

"Good idea. Thank you."

The driver closed the doors, and Oara could lean into them for support. She felt faint, seeing how the city of Arad had changed.

The bus driver's voice jarred her from sadder reflections. "You look familiar."

Oara's first thought was to follow Aurel's advice and refrain from talking to anyone. "I'm visiting the Cureteanu family," she said cautiously.

"Jenica Cureteanu's father is a good friend of my father, and my mother knew his mother, Cornelia. What a special lady she was. I remember her helping my mother make clothes. Everyone in the village admired the clothes she made for herself," said the bus driver.

Oara nodded and smiled. "Everyone in her family knew about that talent. She was gifted." She didn't want to say too much, so she let the bus driver continue.

"It was sad; she passed away so unexpectedly. I wasn't there, but my parents told me about her funeral." He stopped speaking and looked at Oara's face, studying it intently. Suddenly, he gasped. "You are her sister from Bucharest. Jenica mentioned you often after his mother passed away. How is he?"

Oara hoped her face didn't give away how Jenica was doing. Instead, she listened to the driver's happiness over running into someone who knew him, even though it did nothing to help her feel more at ease about the situation.

He didn't notice how her face blanched as he spoke excitedly, talking to her like an old friend. "Last time I saw him, he told me that he was moving to Bucharest to go to university. Wasn't he going to live with you?"

The bus stopped, and without waiting for her to answer his question, he announced, "Mr. Cureteanu's house is right down the street near the water fountain." He pointed in the direction of the house.

Oara walked off the bus and thanked him. "When I see Jenica, who should I tell him was asking about him? I'm sure he'd love to hear from his old friends in the village."

"My name is Vasile, Niculina's son. He'll know me. Have a good evening." With that, he closed the door and headed to his next stop.

Oara watched him leave before walking toward the house. As she stood there, she saw a woman carrying a bucket of water from a fountain. Maria, Jenica's stepmother, was struggling to carry the heavy load. Oara shook her head. *Where is Ionita? Why is he not helping her?*

"Good evening, Maria."

Confused, Maria looked up since she couldn't place the voice. "Dear Oara, is it you? What a surprise! What brings you to us so late at night?"

They stood in the darkened street for a moment, each looking at the other, Maria inquisitive and Oara wondering how she should break the news. It was Maria who spoke first.

"Is Aurel with you?"

Oara nearly gasped her words. "I have news. Is Ionita nearby?" Her face betrayed the gravity of her news, alarming Maria.

"What kind of news? Is there something wrong with Jenica?"

She gestured to Oara to help her carry the bucket of water. It saved her from having to answer anything else until they reached the house.

"Where is Ionita, Momma Maria?"

"Oh, dear, he is where he loves to be most." When they reached the house, Oara saw him sitting on the stairs. Near him was a big bottle of tuica.

"Good evening, Ionita."

The man was barely lucid and barely able to slur, "Oara, what are you doing here?"

Before she could answer, Maria suggested they go inside where it was warm. Oara placed the bucket of water on the kitchen bench while Maria prepared a plate of fresh bread and cheese as well as a shot of tuica to warm Oara up; the second shot was the one that gave Oara the courage to tell them what was happening.

Hearing the news, Ionita drank tuica straight from the bottle before throwing it across the room.

Oara jumped as the bottle shattered against the wall. Maria criticized him. "Enough. You don't need to behave like this in front of Oara."

Ionita growled at her, "I told that boy to stay here and help me run the farm." He glared at Oara and pointed his finger at her. "But no. He wanted to go to college, and you encouraged him. Look what happened. He must be in big trouble to be in that prison. Now tell me, what did he do?"

Oara didn't think she could give an answer that would calm him down, so she simply said, "We don't know yet, but I'm sure that when we hire a lawyer, we'll know the full story."

Ionita glared at her. "What do you mean *we*?"

She tried to backtrack. "Yes, you need to hire a lawyer."

He ignored her. "Maria, tomorrow you are going to Bucharest and find out exactly what is going on."

Ionita stumbled out of the kitchen without saying another word. He'd spent his life giving orders to everyone. Oara despised his arrogant attitude and never understood why her sister loved him. After her death, Ionita was lucky to find Maria, a good wife, and mother to Jenica.

Maria had silently watched throughout the exchange, but she began to cry as soon as Ionita left. "Why is this happening?" Oara rubbed her back and tried to comfort her. Maria covered her face with both hands and cried. When she finally calmed down a little, she approached Oara: "What do you think we should do first?"

"Tomorrow morning, we will take the earliest train to Bucharest. We will look for the best lawyer in town. We are not aware of his charges yet, but Mircea and Aurel speculated that it must be political. We have to try to get him out of there as soon as possible. It won't be easy since lawyers are expensive, especially with the possibly political charges Jenica is facing."

Maria looked at her hands, and a thin smile crept across her face. "Oara, I have money. From my business, I always put some aside for Jenica without Ionita knowing. I offer some of the driver's room and board, and I get paid more than Ionita thinks."

Oara smiled and shook her head affectionately. "You're a bright woman." She'd always liked Jenica's stepmother. Ionita, after he lost his wife, became an alcoholic. He spent most of his time badmouthing her in village bars for no founded reasons. Maria was the one who ran the farm. She stood by him regardless. People in the village admired her for her strength. Besides, she was too busy running the farm to listen to the gossip.

When the roosters started crowing the following day, they were on the first train back to Bucharest. Even though they were quiet most of the trip, lost in thoughts and anxious about everything they needed to do, they occasionally asked questions.

"Oara, I forgot to ask you last night. How'd you find out Jenica is locked in Jilava?"

"I can't believe I didn't tell you. Jenica's girlfriend, Virginia, told us. She's such a nice young lady—from Moldova and a medical student at the university."

Maria looked out the window thoughtfully. "I never thought Jenica would date someone from a different region. He was always so excited to tell people he grew up in Transylvania." A few more miles of country rolled by the window before she spoke again. "I remember one of his friends...I think Mircea. He was also from Moldova."

"That's right; Mircea introduced the pair."

"Well then, she must be a nice young lady."

"I know she loves him and has been looking for him day and night. A couple of days ago, she got a phone call from someone who works at the prison who saw her name and number in the snow next to the word *help*. That's when she came to see us."

Momma Maria started crying again. "Oh my."

"She's been looking for him since November 25."

The train started slowing down as it entered the East Station in Bucharest.

Chapter Eighteen

Vladimir Ciocan stopped by the side of the road to look over the paperwork one more time, even though he'd read the file numerous times. At first, he had refused to take the case. One of his supervisors threw the file on his desk and walked away at the office.

"Take care of this," he had told him.

As he entered the prison and passed the admission desk, he could barely breathe because the smell of mold and urine was so strong it made him sick to his stomach. He read through his biography one more time. He wanted to turn around and leave, but as the door closed behind him, he knew he had to walk down two flights of concrete stairs and go through several more steel doors. Even though Jenica's cellblock was above ground, there were only faint whispers of sunlight in each cell.

Jenica was born in 1931 in the small village of Draut near Arad. His parents were Ionita Cureteanu, a farmer who worked in forestry, and Cornelia Cureteanu, who died in 1949. In 1953, Jenica left Transylvania to study philosophy in Bucharest. Five weeks ago, he had been arrested leaving the faculty dorms. According to the typed summary, the boy's ex-roommate was an informant named Luca Moromete, who reported finding a banned author on Cureteanu's bookshelf. Jenica's case was based on this single piece of evidence. Nothing suggested any involvement with an anticommunist organization named FDC, with any of its leaderships or supporters or their methods of communication.

There weren't any civilians present. However, Adrian Bisu, a field agent suspected of antigovernment activity, was killed while resisting arrest on the same day near the House of the Spark, adjacent to a statue of Stalin.

The report explained that Moromete had plenty of ambition and outward zeal but lacked patience or restraint. Yet he seemed committed to working for the Securitate when he graduated. There wasn't any evidence he would make a good agent. His alcoholism would undoubtedly disqualify him from the program at Baneasa even if he did apply for additional training. Moreover, one piece of intelligence collection was by chance. He sold books at a secondhand shop near the men's dormitory to pay for his drinking habit. When he reported the Iorga material, the agents noticed a bruise over his left eye, thought to be a souvenir from a fight with Cureteanu over stealing Cureteanu's books to pay for his drinking habit.

These facts were brutal for Ciocan to see while looking at the exhausted youth who sat before him. Turning in the Iorga book was only a petty act of revenge for all he knew.

Even though Ciocan felt terrible for him, the possession or sharing of the *Opinions sincères* of Nicolae Iorga was a grave matter. Aurel and Oara Cristiu, Jenica's uncle and aunt, were loyal to the Party. However, he didn't contact them to testify about the boy's character. After Jenica's arrest, he was transferred to the branch office for interrogation but refused to cooperate. The Securitate took him to Jilava to wait for the magistrate to listen to the conspiracy evidence and decide if he was trying to undermine state security. Jenica was sentenced to life without the possibility of parole. Jenica asked if he could contact his family. Ciocan was at the prison to let him know the decision.

Ciocan requested to see Jenica in the interrogation room. When the guards brought him in, he noticed purple bruises and dark red scabs on

Jenica's knuckles and elbows. Ciocan noticed his back seemed stiff. Perhaps he'd been dragged across a rough surface in the last several days.

Since Ciocan wanted to leave the dank prison quickly, his first words were the reason for the visit. Solemnly, regarding Jenica, he said, "I'm afraid I have nothing encouraging to report. Although this is your first offense, the judge believes allowing you to contact your family would unnecessarily risk public safety. The judge denied your request to contact your family. We can discuss this in six months. But I need to let you know that the position is unlikely to change unless an authority retires.

"Mr. Cureteanu, I was informed that you have been on a hunger strike for nine days now. I suggest you stop it immediately. It is not going to work. Please reconsider."

Jenica got up from his chair and walked toward the lawyer, furious. Ciocan stared at him but did nothing.

"Why can't I contact my family? Why am I not allowed to appeal this conviction? You are my lawyer and weren't even at the trial to protect me."

"I'm sorry, but no one told me you were going to be in court that day."

"Sorry? Are you really sorry? Do you understand I am innocent and have done nothing wrong? Tell me why they arrested me leaving my dorm?"

"Mr. Cureteanu, as I informed you earlier, I am here just to let you know that your request to contact your family was denied. I can't give you any other pieces of information."

After seeing the boy's sunken cheeks and listless face, he hoped it had been satisfying for the Securitate to remove such a dangerous element from the world. It was a sad situation, and it seemed like a high price. Naturally, after the uprisings of the previous year, no one wanted students with antisocialist ideas to poison the minds of impressionable young men and women at the university. However, Ciocan couldn't help but note that he didn't understand the sentence of this relatively harmless person who would be behind bars for three or four decades. The informant Andrei Constantinescu, a professor in the university's history department, had done nothing more than turn in a note with a drawing of a flower with three circles in the middle and eight petals and a bizarre message: "Bring your Carpati cigarettes and remember a spark." Again, he considered Luca Moromete, who he thought was a nitwit. He thought again how this note was probably only retaliation, if not against Jenica, then against someone else for something he thought had happened during one of his binges. Many people wanted him eliminated. The directorate did nothing. Luca Moromete would waste valuable time and resources while possibly exposing the operatives to further risk. Everyone knew he was notorious for drinking too much.

Ciocan knocked on the door, signaling to the guards he was ready to go. As he got up from his chair, he asked Jenica, "Do you have any other requests or petitions to make?"

Jenica looked away as if trying to remember something important. Ciocan thought about how his arrest was the only one made in this case. This piece of intelligence from Moromete was beyond useless. A book that Moromete had found on a shelf in Jenica's dorm was the only evidence against him. Jenica was the only one arrested at the dorm. Working hand in hand with Luca Moromete at the university, Professor Constantinescu learned about a meeting planned for Friday night, November 25, the same night that the Securitate decided to arrest Jenica and bring him in for interrogation. A few members from the Securitate went to arrest Jenica, while the majority went to the House of the Spark and teamed up with the police. After receiving the alert, the branch's chief lieutenant dispatched eighteen field agents to the House of the Spark in an attempt to ambush the meeting. The only person they captured was Adrian Bisu. The Securitate killed him; the others escaped.

The lawyer began losing patience and raised his voice, "Mr. Cureteanu, do you have any other requests? Give it some thought. I'll be back in two months."

"I do have one request."

The guard was already inside the room, waiting for the lawyer. However, Ciocan turned back to acknowledge Jenica.

"If I'm not allowed to write, would it be possible to have something to read?"

"I can certainly try," he responded sincerely.

Jenica added, "I'm fond of novels and poetry. How about a volume by Eminescu?"

Ciocan smiled. "It will have to be the censored version. I'll try to bring it to you in a week or two."

Jenica clasped his hands and bowed before the lawyer left the room. The chain around his hands and ankles made the movement difficult.

After Ciocan left, the guards took him back to his cell. Jenica waited for the guards to take the chains from his ankles and hands. They ignored him and left. Jenica waited and waited. They never came back.

When they brought him dinner, Jenica refused to eat again. He felt weak and raised his voice at the guards asking them to remove the chains from his hands and feet. When he started hitting the gate with the chain, they came.

"Did you dare to yell at us?" one said.

They repeatedly struck him with their guns' butts until Jenica collapsed to the floor. Covering his head and face with both hands, he yelled in despair. They kicked him with their boots until he started spitting up blood. They poured his food over him and left the cell.

"Next time, wait till we come to you," one of the guards shouted, closing the cell gate.

Jenica was on the floor the entire night. His body was shivering, and he had a fever when they found him the next day. It was inspection day; the guards unchained his hands and legs and dragged him to the infirmary. He was coughing and spitting out blood. The doctor gave him two big pills and sent him back to his cell a few hours later.

A day later, guards found him unresponsive on the floor. They took him back to the infirmary.

One day, feeling a warm ray of sun embalming his face, he opened his eyes. *I'm still alive*, he thought. Slowly, he tried to move his head from one side to the other. He stopped. Laying on the bed helpless, he recalled moments of his abduction. He was exiting the dorm on November 24 around 7 p.m. Immediately, he heard footsteps behind him. "Jenica Cureteanu…" he heard somebody calling his name. His gut feeling told him to keep walking, and he ignored the voice. A punch in his face made him lose his balance. He saw the lights and heard the tires screech, then he felt scoop and threw in a car. They took him to the police station and started interrogating him. They forced him to confess to crimes of conspiracy against the government. "Monsters, criminals"… angry Jenica tried to get up from the bed, but the sharp pain in his head stopped him. When he opened his eyes the following day, he saw Ciocan waving a book at him. Jenica could barely see him. He was unable to talk or move and slowly closed his eyes. A few days later, he opened his eyes and saw a book near his bed stand. Mihai Eminescu, Luceafarul, he whispered. He hid it under his pillow before anybody could see it.

Chapter Nineteen

When they arrived at Oara's house, Aurel wasn't there. Oara noticed that Maria looked very pale and convinced her to rest for a while. The news of Jenica being in jail devastated her. She agreed to go rest in one of the bedrooms.

"Oh, so soft, so soft," Maria kept repeating to herself until she fell asleep. Oara peeked through the door and watched her sleeping.

"Such a strong woman, beautiful inside and out, with a heart of gold. Married a man like Ionita."

"I don't know what love is," he'd told Oara once.

Ionita reiterated to his friends that Maria was not like Cornelia. Oara thought that he was mistreating Maria and used to tell him straight to his face what she was thinking. Ionita hated her for that. He acted like he wasn't doing anything wrong; Ionita felt he was always right and had to listen to nobody.

* * *

Loud noise blaring from the kitchen disturbed Maria's sleep. Aurel and Oara were fighting. She tried to hear what they were saying.

"I will call Virginia tomorrow morning. Let's all have dinner for now," Oara told Aurel and left the kitchen. Aurel followed her. They crossed paths with Maria, who pretended to come out from the bedroom.

"Aurel, it is good to see you. How have you been?"

"I am much better now that I see you here. Too bad we have to meet in such circumstances."

Maria tried to contain her feelings and act as calmly as she could.

"Aurel, Oara told me what you did. I want to thank you. It took a lot of courage, and I know that in your position, you risk a lot."

"Maria, you know that in other circumstances, I'd be more than happy to let you stay here, but I already risk so much." Aurel put his head down and covered his face with both hands.

"I understand. I don't want to cause more problems for you and Oara. You've both done more than enough, and I am very grateful. I brought you a few bottles of wine from the farm as a small token of my appreciation."

Oara and Maria went into the kitchen and finished preparing dinner. They ate and talked, and the tension seemed to ebb for the rest of the evening.

She left early in the morning. The clock in the living room was showing five-thirty. As Maria rode the bus back to the train station, she was amazed to see how much Bucharest had changed since the last time she and Ionita had visited—lots of tall buildings spread everywhere. Maria sat on one of the benches at the train station, ate bread and cheese from a small handkerchief, and waited until seven o'clock to call Virginia.

* * *

Virginia was just getting ready to leave the apartment when the phone rang.

"Hello? Who is this, please?"

"Virginia? I am Maria, Jenica's stepmother. Oara gave me your number."

Virginia was overjoyed to hear that. Even though she'd never met her, she and Jenica had enjoyed the packages of goodies that Maria sent to him periodically.

"Momma Maria, where are you?"

"I am at the train station. Virginia, I was just wondering if I could stay with you for a couple of days? I hope there is no trouble for you."

"No, not at all. And yes, you are more than welcome to stay with me. I'll just have to ask Doina, my roommate, if you can use her room. She stays with her boyfriend, Mircea, most of the time. I am sure you've heard of him. I can come to get you from the train station; let's meet outside the front door in about thirty minutes?"

"It's been a while since I visited Bucharest, and it has changed so much. I appreciate you doing this for me."

"I'll be there in thirty minutes." At first, Virginia was worried about not attracting attention since she noticed being followed, but she was also overjoyed; she was getting closer to helping Jenica.

* * *

A young woman with long, black hair wearing a beautiful blue dress and an edelweiss pin on the left side of her chest got Maria's attention.

"Virginia?"

The young lady turned around.

"Momma Maria. Everything is all right. I spoke with Doina already."

"Thank you, dear."

On the bus, Maria asked Virginia, "The pin, the edelweiss flower—it's a gift from Jenica, right?"

Virginia nodded and looked at the pin and then at Maria. "Is it yours?"

"Oh no, dear. It was Jenica's mother's favorite pin. I'm surprised that Jenica hasn't told you yet."

"He gave it to me at Christmas…"

How nice, Maria thought.

When they arrived at the apartment, to their surprise, Mircea and Doina were waiting. They all greeted each other and then went into the kitchen and sat around the table to talk while Doina prepared some warm tea for everybody.

Mircea was the first to talk. "Momma Maria, I've contacted some of my friends' lawyers. I tried to find out more information about the events near the House of the Spark a few months ago. I couldn't find out much, as there was no news among the faculty about an ambush in front of the Stalin statue. I did find one of the best lawyers in town, whom I think you should meet with."

"Can you take me to his office? I am afraid I can't wait any longer. I have to find out how to get Jenica out of that place."

"I have to go back to work, but I've explained to Virginia how to get there. It's really not far from here."

* * *

When Maria and Virginia arrived at the office of well-known lawyer and native Transylvanian Alexandru Ardelean, he was not there. His secretary informed them that he was at the courthouse, but she did expect him back in a couple of hours. Maria mentioned Mircea's name.

The secretary smiled at her. "Mircea Greceanu. I will tell him that he referred you."

They were ready to exit when Maria almost bumped into a very tall man wearing an impeccable black suit, a white shirt, and a tie with the Romanian flag's red, yellow, and blue. The secretary called Maria back and told her to have a seat.

A few minutes later, she invited Maria into the office. Virginia stayed outside.

"Mrs. Cureteanu, my secretary, just informed me that Mircea Greceanu referred you. Is that right?"

"Yes, sir." Maria stopped for a moment to catch her breath. "Are you the best lawyer in town, Mr. Ardelean?"

The lawyer started laughing. "Oh, I'm not sure about that. I'm not aware of my reputation, but I like the idea. Tell me, what can I do for you?"

Almost an hour later, Maria came out, wiping her face with her handkerchief. She didn't say much but began walking quickly. Virginia followed her.

"Can we stop at the church for a while? The *White Church*," said Maria, pointing toward it.

"How did it go?" Virginia asked her.

Maria did not answer and just shook her head while tears poured down her face. She managed to open the big, wooden door of the church. They both sat on one of the benches. Maria wiped her tears, then told her, "He explained to me how the system works and that it might take years before he can do something for Jenica; as for now, he will try to get a hold of his file. He said that it's tough to have access to that kind of file since the Securitate keeps them well hidden.

"So that's the plan for now. The lawyer will try to find and look into his file to see what evidence they have against him. I wanted to offer him money, but he refused it."

"Mircea told me he helped many people benevolently. Mr. Ardelean was his first mentor after he finished college. 'If I could think of anyone who might be able to help Jenica, it has to be Mr. Ardelean,' he told me the other day. Even though the Securitate tried to cause him problems, he knows how to play them. Mircea says Jenica's life is in the best hands. Now we just have to wait and see."

"He told me to give him a month to start the process. Can you take me to the train station now?"

Virginia agreed.

* * *

On the long ride back home, Maria thought of her conversation with Ionita about Jilava. "Don't spend your time and money, woman! I've never heard about anybody able to get out alive from that place. That place is hell. It is worse than a concentration camp. I am just letting you know that you'll fight a battle that is already lost."

"So you just want me to forget about him? What is wrong with you? How can you be so coldhearted? Jenica is your son, and even though he's not my biological son, I love him too. I don't care what you think; I am not giving up on Jenica. He doesn't deserve to be there."

Ionita told her that even though he wasn't pleased to know that his son was in jail, it was not a surprise for him to find out that he had gotten into trouble. He admitted that the boy was hardworking—well organized, intelligent, and a keen learner. Jenica had a habit of forgetting his manners when he was angry or vexed. Frequently, he got carried away to the point of abusiveness and self-abandon. Ionita anticipated that once he'd been at the university, away from the supervision and guidance of his own family, it was only a matter of time before he would get into trouble. Was it so un-likely that he should encounter a provocative set of ideas or get entangled with the wrong crowd and take it all a bit too far?

"Do what you want, but don't ask me to help. I told that boy a long time ago to stay here," concluded Ionita.

Maria was fed up listening to his excuses. Later that evening, she was back at her house in Draut village. As expected, Ionita was sitting on the house stairs with his "best friend"—tuica.

Chapter Twenty

Mircea decided to pay a visit to Eugene, Jenica's roommate. He wasn't in his room. Mircea realized he'd still be in class for a bit longer. He'd taken the same program a few years back, so he was familiar with the schedule. He left a note for Eugene and went to La Rotunda.

A short time later, Eugene arrived at the bar. Mircea took a sip of his mineral water, pausing so he wouldn't say something he'd regret. The two firmly shook hands.

Jenica's roommate looked clean-shaven and well rested. Mircea resented him for his blasé manner—he looked like nothing was wrong in the world. After all, Mircea, alongside Doina and Virginia, had lost many nights of sleep since finding out that Jenica was in Jilava. However, he did notice that Eugene's socks didn't match. Since he was usually so meticulous about his appearance, Mircea knew something was off.

"Sorry to keep you waiting."

"Eh, I've only been here for a minute or two." Mircea took another sip of his mineral water.

"Your note sounded like you needed to talk about something important. I have an evening lecture to go to, but it's not for another hour." Eugene shrugged and ordered a beer.

"I've gotten used to seeing you with Jenica this time of the day," he told Mircea. "Have you been out of town for a while?"

"No, just busy with work." Mircea got straight to the point. "Did you know that Jenica's locked up at Jilava?"

It was at that moment that Eugene's calm demeanor cracked. Although he knew very little about criminal courts and the Securitate, like most people in Bucharest, he knew that Jilava was one of the worst prisons. Most of the staff were uneducated Romanian peasants. Often, they beat and humiliated the prisoners. Stunned at this revelation, Eugene shuddered, imagining Jenica in that grotesque place.

"What were his charges?"

"We weren't able to find out yet, but it must be for political reasons. Jenica's sentence was life in prison without the possibility of parole."

Eugene looked disturbed. He'd heard about the political prisoners at Jilava charged and put on trial in absurd, theatrical showroom demonstrations, cut off from any contact with lawyers. He'd heard they were never permitted to speak with their families or send or receive correspondence or packages. It was rare for the authorities to acknowledge imprisoned men or declare the crimes they had tried them with, so Jilava became an effortless place to make someone disappear.

Eugene took another gulp of beer and continued, "I think Luca had something to do with this. At least I have my suspicions."

"Jenica's ex-roommate?"

"Yes. Gut feeling: he had something to do with this. But we'll never know because he was hit by a car."

"This is strange." Mircea looked at his watch. "Listen, Eugene. I have to go. I wanted to tell you what was going on and to let you know that Virginia and I will be coming by to get Jenica's things since Friday is the last day of school."

"No problem. I'll be there every day until Sunday. Feel free to come and retrieve his belongings. I hope he can find a way to get out of there. Jenica is a good guy, and we got along well."

Mircea muttered his thanks and left without saying another word.

A few days later, he returned with Virginia to the dorm and boxed up Jenica's things. After they packed everything, they looked one more time around the room. On the side of the shelf was a picture of Virginia. When he removed the photo, Mircea saw a small keyhole behind it. Virginia pulled a hairpin from her hair and stuck it in and out. The door opened, and inside they found Iorga's book from Tony.

Mircea's eyes opened wide. "I would never have thought to look there. Good job, Virginia."

She was holding the book close to her chest and closed her eyes.

Chapter Twenty-One

On the last autumn day, Maria and Ionita finally received a letter from Jenica's lawyer telling them to come to Bucharest. Maria was on the first train out; Ionita opted not to go with her.

The long train ride gave Maria too much time to think. Even though she tried to focus on the scenery rushing by her to calm her nerves, all she wanted was answers and for Jenica to be set free. Ionita had started another fight when she asked him to go with her. He couldn't rouse himself from his drunken stupor even for a few days to focus on his son. Her sadness and anger were taxing, giving her the first pains of a headache. Several hours later, she stepped off the train into Bucharest's crowded Northern Railway Station. Virginia was waiting for her.

"Momma Maria." Virginia choked back tears, seeing the effect of the last few months on Jenica's stepmother. Her depression had caused many sleepless nights, and her appetite was almost nonexistent. Every thought led her back to Jenica and Jilava.

"I hope the lawyer has some good news for us. Would you come with me tomorrow?" Virginia was happy to hear that.

"Are you sure? Why didn't Jenica's father bother to come to talk with the lawyer?"

"It's a long story, Virginia. Ionita was very young when his father died of leukemia. Since then, he's believed that books killed his father. His father read a lot and barely spent time with his family. Ionita never liked to read and tried to prove to his mother that he could make a living without going to college. Unfortunately, Ionita disagreed with the idea of Jenica going to college. Anyway, it's a sad story."

Virginia was stared at her the whole time she was talking. She thought of Jenica, who never mentioned his struggle with his father. She rushed and set the table for her and Maria. Maria opened a small bottle with tuica and poured in two little glasses.

"We both need a boost," she said jokingly.

They ate roasted eggplant salad with bread.

*　*　*

That night, Virginia was unable to sleep. She looked out the window into the quiet night, thinking about how Jenica probably hadn't seen a sunrise or a starry night in months. She could see the White Church through her tears. The church looked like a beacon of hope in the moonlight. It was a place her father often visited when he came to Bucharest.

She rose from the bed and went into the kitchen. Maria was sitting at the table drinking a warm cup of tea.

"Momma Maria, are you OK?"

"Yes, I just wasn't able to fall asleep. It's been so many months since Jenica was arrested. I wonder if he is still alive. Maybe the lawyer just wants to let us know that he is dead."

Virginia walked toward her. "Jenica is not dead. He is fighting; remember, he risked everything to let us know that he is in jail."

"You're probably right, Virginia. But all the rumors of abuse from the guards and the management, not to mention the food…How can anybody survive in that place? You know Jenica is not that strong." After a moment of silence, Maria got up from her chair. "We'd better go to sleep."

The next morning, they set off down Victory Avenue, which people compared with the Champs-Élysées in Paris. Usually, they would have loved the stroll, but they were fighting against a strong wind as they made their way down the avenue. Luckily, they didn't have to go very far. They agreed to stop and pray at the church before the appointment with the lawyer. Soon they were able to see the church. They rushed in. Virginia looked around in admiration at the splendid iconostases that decorated the church's walls. *What a beautiful and peaceful place*, she thought. She recalls one of her last conversations with her father.

"Virginia, I badly scarred my soul on the road of my life. Please don't ever give up, no matter what life might throw at you. I will look down from heaven and pray for you."

"I promise, father," she whispered.

She looked at Maria, praying in front of the Saint Nicholas statue. Virginia knelt and joined her in prayer. They spent some time in front of the statue until they both felt strong enough to get up.

"I don't know about you, Virginia, but I think I am ready to go face Jenica's lawyer."

"I'm ready too." They both rose and left the building. With each step they took, their confidence grew more assertive.

In no time, they reached Mr. Ardelean's office. He was waiting.

"Is Mr. Cureteanu coming also?" the lawyer asked.

Maria put her head down. "No, sir, but I want you to meet Jenica's girlfriend, Virginia Gemanar."

"Glad to finally meet you. I've heard a lot about you. Let's all sit and start our meeting." Mr. Ardelean looked discreetly at his watch.

"I have good and bad news. The good news: I was able to see Jenica in prison. He is not doing too well, but he is alive and fighting for his life every day. The bad news: I couldn't get Jenica's file from his lawyer to see their evidence against him. Jenica's lawyer, a man by the name of Vladimir Ciocan, has vanished. He was the last to look at Jenica's file. I petitioned the court; I could not set a date in court to appeal his sentence. They told me to wait without giving me a specific reason."

"But how is it possible for Jenica's file to disappear?" Virginia recalled her conversation with Mircea about Adrian Bisu's missing file.

"I suspect that the Securitate got hold of it and hid it. It's just speculation, of course."

"No." Virginia shook her head. "It's the truth. In a few days or months, Jenica will vanish from Jilava, and there will be no trace of him. That's how they did it with—" Furious, she stopped talking.

"That's how they did with…whom, Virginia?"

"Adrian Bisu, sir."

"Never heard of that name. Can you tell me more about him?"

"It's useless; he's already dead and vanished without a trace."

"We'll talk about him some other time if you like." The lawyer looked at his watch. "Unfortunately, I have to be at the courthouse in about thirty minutes. Momma Maria, I will contact you as soon as I can find out more about Jenica's file."

He shook hands with Maria and Virginia and rushed out the door.

Maria got up from her chair and almost lost her balance. Virginia offered her support.

"Are you OK?"

"Yes, let's go to the apartment."

They walked back without saying a word to each other.

Doina was at the apartment. Virginia made a subtle sign to her not to talk and then helped Maria to her room.

"I would like to be alone for a while," Maria told her.

"Certainly, I'll be in the kitchen if you need anything."

Virginia grabbed her coat and signaled to Doina to follow her. They went down the street to a small cafeteria and sat at one of the tables. She then gave Doina details of everything that had happened in the lawyer's office.

Doina was shocked. "All this abuse. So if they don't have a file on him, they should let him free."

"It's not that simple, Doina. I have to go back; I am worried that Maria might wake up and wonder where I am. She hasn't said too much since we left the lawyer's office. I'll keep in touch." She kissed Doina on the cheek and rushed back to her apartment.

* * *

Almost six months had passed before Maria received another letter from Jenica's lawyer.

After returning from work, Ionita took off his jumpsuit and splashed himself outside. He washed his hands with a soap Maria had made that dissipated the smell of wood chips and sap. In the kitchen, he opened a big bottle of tuica. Maria was warming a loaf of bread in the oven and dropped a fistful of parsley into a soup of potatoes. She looked toward Ionita. "I got a letter from Jenica's lawyer; he wants us to go see him."

"Hmm."

The husband and wife had been avoiding each other's glances, and there was still tension between them. They hadn't recovered yet from the argument when Maria first asked him to go with her to Bucharest.

"I'm not going, but you can go ahead and do what you want. You're wasting your time on that spoiled kid. His sorry situation is his own fault."

Maria called Virginia to let her know that she was coming to the city. Contrary to Ionita's remark that he thought Virginia had lost her mind from despair, Maria knew she was a very smart and kind person and was determined to help Jenica get out of jail.

* * *

Maria brought two bags full of goodies for the lawyer and handed them to his secretary.

"A gift for Mr. Ardelean."

"That is very kind of you, Momma Maria."

"Momma Maria, Virginia, good to see you again. I have some news for you. I reached out to a group of lawyers who could run circles around the judge. I was finally able to find Jenica's file. Since receiving the file, I've had problems with the Securitate. They are hiding something. I was almost run over by a car. They throw rocks at the windows of my house. The phone rings all night long."

"Are you sure it's the Securitate doing these horrible things to you?" Maria was shocked.

"Oh yeah. Even the judge advised me, in private, to give up on Jenica's case. But enough about me; let's talk about Jenica's conviction. There is a testimony on his file from the person who turned him in. Virginia, are you aware of a student by the name of Luca Moromete?"

"Yes, he was Jenica's first roommate."

"I read in Jenica's file that he retrieved a book from Jenica's bedroom about Nicolae Iorga, the historian banned by the Securitate; I am sure you've heard of him. Another Securitate informer from the university, Professor Constantinescu, wrote a statement against Jenica. He suspected Jenica's involvement with an anticommunist organization called FDC."

Virginia didn't know what to answer.

"Sir, I started suspecting Luca a while back because of his sneaky behavior, and rumors spread around the university that he was a Securitate informer, but it didn't cross my mind that Jenica would be sentenced based on a testimony given by Luca. Everybody knew that he was a severe alcoholic. As far as the book goes, I found it hidden in his bedroom, so I am not sure what book Luca turned in to the Securitate."

"He framed him. It looks like he found a book by Iorga and turned it in to the Securitate, stating that it was Jenica's book. They can't prove that it was or was not his book, and Luca can't testify because he is dead. But I might be able to appeal this sentence since there is not enough evidence on Jenica's file.

"The good thing is Jenica is still fighting. As long as he is not giving up, we will not give up. It's not easy to fight against those monsters. The Securitate is active all over the country and uses its power in the most mischievous ways. As for now, the best thing is to avoid any confrontation with them.

"I heard rumors that Jenica's lawyer, Mr. Ciocan, was found dead, shot in the back of the head a few weeks ago near Baneasa Forest."

"Do you think that the Securitate is to blame?" Virginia asked him.

"I do not doubt it."

Maria started crying. "Mr. Ardelean, you have to do something, please."

"Ciocan was one of the lawyers who fought against the Securitate and was forced to take over Jenica's file. I'll try my best, but I can't promise you anything. I will try to persuade the judge to reduce his prison time or grant him parole—or at least to allow his family to contact him and exchange letters."

He walked Maria and Virginia to the door.

"As long as he is alive, there's a chance; let's not lose hope. Goodbye for now."

As they exited the office, they could hear the shouts of pedestrians and drivers honking their horns off in the distance. The motorcade of the president was shuffling down the street.

Chapter Twenty-Two

"Virginia, let's see the president."

Virginia barely had the chance to say something when Maria rushed toward the crowd. She was moving fast, pushing through the crowd, sprinting down the sidewalk. People stood shoulder to shoulder, barely able to wave the flags they were holding. Suddenly, the energy in the crowd shifted. Maria had dashed through the public and in front of the president's car. Her eyes frightened the group, who tried to flee in all directions. The president's car narrowly missed Maria, who stood in front of the vehicle. The tires screeched, and a group of people who spilled off the crowded sidewalk screamed as they were almost hit. A few of the Securitate guards accompanying the motorcade intervened right away and wrestled Maria to the ground while others ensured the president was safe.

With a mix of shock and curiosity, people watched the drama unfold. Maria struggled against the iron grip of the guards, repeating, "Mr. President, sir! Mr. President! Please let me talk with you. Please!"

"Shut up! If you don't stop, we'll shoot you," one of the guards yelled at her.

She ignored him and continued her plea. The handcuffs started to cut into her skin. She was aware of the pain but kept yelling, trying to get the president's attention. Besides, the metal cutting into her wrists was nothing compared to the pain she felt hearing the terrible news about Jenica.

She'd tried everything else and knew this was her last option. She continued her plea, turning her tears into a shout. "Mr. President, help me! My son is locked in Jilava!" Her voice got louder as she struggled against the Securitate. She knew she only had seconds for him to hear her and maybe, just maybe, decide to help her.

"My son is in Jilava! Help him!"

The police pulled her to the ground. The men started to drag her away roughly. The commotion was dying down as people nearby who'd seen what happened were standing there in disbelief. A few women were crying, and others stood with dumbfounded expressions. Their flags lowered, and they no longer thought about the celebration.

Maria continued her litany as she was being pulled away. "Mr. President, my son is locked at Jilava! Please help him!"

The president's car was about to pull away.

"Stop the car now!" he bellowed.

The tires screeched. People watching the scene started moving further back.

Unsure why this woman's pleas affected him so much, the president signaled one of the Securitate guards to approach the car.

"What is going on?" he demanded. "Was the woman who almost killed herself saying something about Jilava?"

"Yes, sir. The woman wants a reprieve for her son, who's locked in Jilava."

The Securitate was worried that this event would call for more civil unrest. They were angry, wondering how someone could be so stupid to think that the president would care about her son.

They spoke with the president coldly as he listened intently. He still didn't understand why her pleas had affected him like this. Perhaps it was because he instinctively knew she wasn't someone who wanted to act against him, just a woman who feared for her child. Or maybe he recalled his experiences being locked in prison.

As they spoke, the president nodded his head solemnly and paused a few moments before speaking. "I want to talk with her. Have them bring her to my office first thing in the morning." Without another word, he signaled the driver to move on.

* * *

The Securitate threw her in a chair before starting the interrogation.

"What is your name?" One of the Securitate officers regarded her icily. He didn't care who she was, only why she had jeopardized the president's life.

"My name is Maria Cureteanu." She stared them down, feeling resolute that this was the only way to help her stepson.

Later, a tall man in a dark suit strode toward her. He was angry at the audacity of this simple peasant. He looked at her unfeelingly and demanded, "Is your son's incarceration the only reason you jumped in front of the president's car?" He emphasized his feeling that it was a stupid reason for causing the unnecessary disturbance.

"Yes, sir."

"Do you realize how many people you could have killed or injured with your little stunt?" He wanted her to feel bad. Truthfully, he didn't care why she did it. She wouldn't get to see the president if he had his way. He couldn't understand why the president had a soft spot for a woman like this.

"I do," Maria answered him softly, realizing she hadn't thought about all the people in the crowd. She felt selfish, but it was overshadowed by gratitude that the president had agreed to meet with her. Not wanting them to see the slight smile, she looked down at the ground. The Securitate officers present in the room took this as a sign of submission.

The man in the black suit didn't need any other information and hoped she wasn't lying. Silently, he walked out of the room to speak with the

Securitate at the scene. Maria sat in the interrogation room. The adrenaline had worn off, and she became aware of the intense pain on her wrists. Nonetheless, if Maria could get the president to listen and help Jenica, it would all be worth it. She whispered a prayer in the moments before the Securitate officer came back into the room.

The door opened, and a Securitate officer came and took her handcuffs off.

"You can go now, but you'd better be back here tomorrow morning. I don't know why the president agreed to meet with you. I'll take you to him. Don't be late."

"Thank you, sir." She exited the room, repeating, "Thank you."

Outside the station, Virginia was waiting for her. Maria rushed to her and collapsed in her arms. Everything that had happened over the last several hours had drained her, yet knowing tomorrow she'd meet with the president gave her a new sense of purpose.

* * *

The entire city was covered in a layer of cruel, nipping frost the day Maria went to see the president. One of his servants offered her a cup of warm tea.

"Mr. President, Maria Cureteanu is here, sir."

"Who?" the president asked.

"The woman who jumped in front of your car yesterday, sir."

"Oh yes, I'll be there in a moment."

The president got up from his office chair and walked toward a small table. He picked up a silver picture frame. It was the portrait of a woman who, on the face, looked very close to the one of Maria Cureteanu. In the picture was the president's mother with the president when he was about fifteen years old.

When the president entered the room, Maria became overwhelmed. She got up from her chair but looked down at the floor. The president invited her to have a seat. He looked at her for a while and said nothing.

"You are a brave woman…Maria. Is that right?"

"Yes, sir."

"So, tell me, what happened to your son?"

"My son was arrested while exiting his dorm almost a year ago…."

Fifteen minutes later, Maria left the president's office. The Securitate took her back to the police station. Virginia was outside the station, waiting for her.

"What did the president tell you?"

"He promised that they would look into Jenica's file."

A whole week had passed since then, and they'd received no news. Virginia, Mircea, and Doina had begun to accept that they would never see their beloved friend again, but Maria guarded a quiet hope.

Then they got the call. A new magistrate had taken over the case, and this time, Mr. Ardelean was in the courtroom defending Jenica.

Virginia waited outside the courtroom. Her mind returned to the day Maria jumped in front of the president's car. They had interrogated Maria at the police station for hours until they concluded that she was reckless and unbounded. Yet it was clear that the woman was in her right mind and far from trying to hurt anyone; all she had meant to do was attract the president's attention and see if he, of all people, could petition to save her stepson. She agreed to place her name on any number of registries and commit to all sorts of further acts of service to the Party.

"Your Honor, I am here to represent Mr. Jenica Cureteanu, accused of conspiracy against the Communist Party. His conviction is based entirely on one piece of evidence—a copy of a banned book—submitted to the Securitate by an informant who is not available to testify: Luca Moromete is dead."

The magistrate heard the testimony, looked at the evidence, agreed that there was insufficient evidence for Jenica's convictions, and overturned his sentence. Jenica was moved to temporary detention within a few days and prepared to return home.

The group of friends was ecstatic.

"Momma Maria, you are a courageous woman," Mircea told her and gave her a big hug.

The next day, Mr. Ardelean called her into his office.

"Mrs. Cureteanu, I have to tell you, in my entire career, I have never met a woman as courageous as you are. I hope Jenica knows how lucky he is to have you."

"I did what I had to do to save his life."

"And you did; you saved his life," the lawyer told her. "What you did was a smart, courageous, and hazardous thing to do, but in the end, it paid off. Jenica will be released this Friday."

* * *

Early Friday morning, Maria, Virginia, Doina, and Mircea went to Jilava prison to pick up Jenica. They waited almost four hours outside the prison gate. Mircea and Maria went to ask why it was taking so long. The guard told Maria that the director wanted to speak with her. The black walls of the prison frightened her. *No*, she began repeating to herself, *Jenica is not dead*. They told her to have a seat inside the freezing and mold-smelly room. She waited for another hour until, finally, a man dressed in a uniform entered the room.

"Are you Mrs. Cureteanu, Jenica Cureteanu's mother?"

"Yes, yes, sir."

"I have to inform you that he was transferred this morning to the sanatorium. He has tuberculosis and needs to stay away for a while."

Maria started crying and thought about the ambulance they had seen exiting the prison that morning while waiting outside. Nobody came to let them know that Jenica was transferred to the sanatorium. She was disappointed hearing the news but happy that Jenica was alive and out of Jilava.

"He is alive and out of here," Virginia breathed with relief upon hearing the news.

Later that night, Maria was on the train back to Draut. She thought of the future.

I have to find a way to bring Ionita and Jenica back together. It is foolish to stay mad at each other, but it's going to take some time, she thought, knowing how stubborn both men could be.

It would take another year till Jenica would be ready to meet his family and friends again. The treatment for tuberculosis took all of those months. Again Virginia feared for his life since Jenica had the same diagnosis as her father years back. This time around, there were medications available to treat his illness, and Jenica could recover completely.

* * *

December 1958 (one and a half years later).

"Jenica, where are you?" someone from the crowd shouted. Everybody was ready to open the presents.

Jenica got up from the recliner and went into the living room. It was Christmas Day, and they all gathered at Tony's house to celebrate— Virginia, Mircea, Doina, Professor Flueras, Tony, and others.

"Ardelene, come over here; let's take a picture all together," said Mircea to Jenica.

Jenica handed Mircea a white envelope. "Merry Christmas, Moldovene, and thank you again for everything you and Doina did for me."

Mircea looked at the envelope before he opened it. "What's this—you trying to bribe me to do something for you?"

Mircea opened the envelope, shook his head, and looked at Jenica. They both started laughing, getting everybody's attention.

"I have an idea; I'll tell you later," said Mircea, hiding the envelope in his pocket.

They took several pictures together.

"Jenica, why don't you take a picture with Virginia?" Doina suggested.

"Oh, isn't that nice?" said Mircea, looking at the couple. He kissed Doina on the cheek and then walked toward the kitchen, mumbling, "Once upon a time, there was an Ardelean boy who fell in love with a Moldovan girl…." Virginia, Doina, and Jenica looked at each other and started laughing.

* * *

A few hours later, in Tony's basement, Jenica, Professor Flueras, Victor, Alexandru, and, this time, Mircea gathered.

"Welcome to the House of Spark!" Tony announced. "As we all know, the Soviet troops left Romania, but our fight is not over yet. We are going to continue to fight against the Communists, against this system that doesn't believe in fundamental human rights, freedom of speech, and religion."

Once again, Jenica and his coconspirators at FDC gathered to start a new project to ask the ideological questions they were afraid to ask two years ago.

"The fight continues," Tony concluded. "Let's all continue to celebrate Christmas. Jenica and I will contact everybody soon."

* * *

When she saw the statue of the Godfather, Virginia removed her gloves to adjust the clip of her ponytail. Then she immediately put them back on. The sky was still gray in the early morning, and while the days were supposed to be getting longer, everyone was still wearing heavy coats, hats, and scarves out on the street and were bending over to block the wind from numbing their exposed cheeks. It was almost too cold to check her watch, though Virginia was anxious that she would be late for a concert at the Athenaeum yet again.

Feeling sore calves from her brisk walk across the neighborhood, Virginia sat on one of the benches near the statue to rest her legs. Looking at the statue, she fiddled with her tiny brooch. She was excited and unable to keep still.

"Quite impressive," someone commented next to her.

Virginia smiled at her. "You know, I wanted to ask you…the tickets for the concert, it was you—"

"But this time, it was your husband," Doina told her. "And Mircea planned it all out."

Doina had suggested that the entire chain of events had been a divinely inspired test of faith for Jenica's friends. And while Mircea doubted this, Virginia admitted that her ideas about destiny and heavenly guidance would never be the same again. As she stood in front of the bronze statue of Eminescu, it was hard to shake the sensation of being caught in a strange, miraculous dream. She could imagine Jenica returning to his studies, graduating, but none of this was more real than the images of him growing old in Jilava prison for decades to come.

In another moment, Virginia felt a tap on her shoulder and turned around. It was Jenica holding a bag of chocolate candies with the name *Capezzoli di Venere* (Nipples of Venus) written in florid script on the packaging.

"Happy anniversary," he said. "We've finally made it to a matinee at the Athenaeum. I am so sorry to have made you wait."

Mircea pretended to clear his throat, interrupting them. "Look. They just opened the doors. Let's find some good seats. After you all," he said with a bow.

Virginia and Jenica gazed at each other while walking toward the entrance.

"Oh, Jenica, these are delicious…" Virginia rushed to eat one more candy before they all stepped inside the Athenaeum.

Acknowledgements

I always remember the words: Things happen in our lives, and we don't have control over it, but that is why we have each other to help us go through these moments to know that most of the time, it's a light at the end of the tunnel.

Even though I experience a lot of struggle down the road of writing this book, I have the support of some outstanding members of my family and friends.

I would like to thank: my parents and my grandparents in heaven. Your extraordinary story was an inspiration for my book. Thank you to my oldest son, Trace, who encourage me to write and tell the story. Thank you to my friend, Karen, for always seeing the positive and the potential in me.

Thank you to Alexandra Lapointe and her team of editors at Palmetto Lora, Scott, and Albert. Each of you brought a unique and valuable point of view on helping polish my book. Also, a special thanks to Palmetto's people behind the scene who help create the cover, the book's format, etc. I admire your hard work and dedication. **I thank you all from the bottom of my heart.**

Special thanks to my wonderful friend and designer of my cover Teresa Jenellen. You are simply amazing, and I am happy that we crossed the path in life.

I am grateful to all of you who help me down my journey. I hope that every person interested in reading this book will remember something about the country I was born in and become famous thanks to Bran Stoker's story Dracula.

About the Author

Luminita Laflash was born in Bucharest, Romania, during President Ceausescu's leadership. Her father, a philosophy professor, was a protective and affectionate man and took his four children on many trips around the country. Unfortunately, he drank heavily and was subject to rapid mood swings. Luminita pushed through her unhappy childhood and fought to achieve her dream. In 1997 she immigrated to the United States. Far away from the land of her birth, she started a new life. Today, she is the proud mother of three children and two grandchildren. When she struggles, she always remembers her mother's encouraging words, "The sun will rise again for us one day."